Tim Wells is made of regga
and Leyton Orient FC.

SHINE ON ME

Tim Wells

unbound

First published in 2022

Unbound
Level 1, Devonshire House, One Mayfair Place, London W1J 8AJ
www.unbound.com

Text design by PDQ Digital Media Solutions Ltd.

A CIP record for this book is available from the British Library

ISBN 978-1-80018-156-4 (paperback edition)
ISBN 978-1-80018-158-8 (ebook)

Printed in Great Britain by CPI Group (UK)

1 3 5 7 9 8 6 4 2

For Lucinda Jessop

With special thanks to Bob Wells

CHAPTER 1

The eye of the deer was level with that of the wolf. Flat on its side, the deer lay with the wolf's jaws gripping its throat; with every flex the teeth bit deeper and sliced flesh. Blood ran into the grass and turned the soil to a dark red mud. Steam rose from the haunches of the deer as its breathing slowed and ebbed to finality.

There was no fear in the eye of the deer. That had passed and it was resigned to this fate. The yellow eyes of the wolf showed no emotion. A flat knowledge was contained in him. He, too, was resigned to the way of things; a hunger, that need to be satiated, and the killing of the weaker to do so.

The deer had spent its life in the safety and ease of Clissold Park, Stoke Newington, a green space in the heart of London. A pleasant enough place but along with the broad oak trees and calming lake there were the teenage fumblings that took place under the trees and the tales of Dr Crippen meeting his mistress on the ornamental bridge. The shadowed earth beneath one particular oak was littered with cider bottles. This was where the local leather-jacketed punks came to do their punking.

Joe Bovshover had chosen the park. He knew that this full moon he'd become wolf. He knew the deer in the park would make easy prey. The deer lived simply and were soft; there was no wildness to these city animals, but there was in Joe.

Joe knew that there was a beast in him. Not the Leslie Phillips after a few Martinis sort, but the red in tooth and claw. The DJ at the last gig he'd been to had spun the Black Art 7 'Wolf Out Deh' and his heart sank, even as, unconsciously, his tongue had worked around his canines. The howl on the Upsetter production a cold hand on his shoulder. There'd already been several killings committed by this beast. They'd been put down to a lesser animal, a thug called Kessler who'd been jailed for them. But Joe now knew the grim truth. No onism for he. Every full moon he turned; became a slavering, remorseless, relentless werewolf.

Knowing that he had no control over himself when a wolf, he'd decided to loose himself near to easy prey. That at least might spare another innocent from a savage death. He'd petted and fed deer in the park since he was a kid, it was a popular place for local families, but better one of the deer should become meat than a person.

Charles Manby Smith's book *Curiosities of London Life*, from 1853, notes of the city: 'London is something else besides a wilderness – indeed it is everything else. It is a great world, containing a thousand little worlds in its bosom; and pop yourself down in any quarter you will, you are sure to find yourself in the centre of some peculiar microcosm distinguished from all others by features more or less characteristic.'

Joe had been bitten by Lene Lovich at a Hope and Anchor gig and since had become a werewolf. It seemed fantastical, yet it happened, and kept happening. Joe now knew this; his girlfriend's mate, Mark Hazell, also knew. Mark had 'the gift' and was sensitive to the strange and weird.

Joe lived on the edge of east London, not the East End, but just off Stamford Hill. Running through the manor was the long Roman road, known to those conquerors as Ermine Street, that ran from Bishopsgate in the City to York. For some it was a highway for commerce and culture to spread, for others it was a spear that lanced the heart of London. Tacitus wrote about Britain under the Romans in the *Agricola*: 'And so the population was gradually led into the demoralising temptations of arcades, baths, and sumptuous banquets. The unsuspecting Britons spoke of such novelties as "civilisation", when in fact they were only a feature of their enslavement.'

Joe was not a man at C&A, Romans in Britain would not put his bum on a seat, he was a glass half-full lad but all the same it wasn't Cinzano. He was cropped hair, the heavy bass kill of dub reggae, Dr Martens, hard work, the roll collars of button-down shirts and striving for independence. Yet every month he lost his will to the pull of the full moon.

*

The circle had been chalked on the ground of a cellar in Shoreditch, and the smudge of smoke from burning charcoal spread an acrid smell through the dank air. Coal dust from when the building knew more prosperous times was still in the joins of the flags on the floor.

A bell rang, thinly, three times to indicate that this temporal world was now beyond. Inside the circle a robed figure leaned forward and whispered barely audible words. As the occultist Eliphas Levi opined, the demands of the craft were 'To know, to dare, to will, to keep silent'.

It might seem bizarre that here in London, in 1980, witches still practised their rites. But London has lived through fire, plague and war with people praying to live through them all, and in our mess of streets people have turned to every deity and power there is.

During the fourteenth century girls made a renaissance of their beauty by using belladonna. The word means beautiful lady in Italian, and drops of it were used to dilate their eyes and give them the appearance of huge black pools to drown in. The plant is poisonous, and it took a knowing person to prepare the cosmetic safely. As a poison, both Livia, the wife of Augustus, and Locusta, Nero's favoured poisoner, put its properties to their will. Witches not only made money and power from the plant's cosmetic properties but made their flying ointment from it.

From the torn ground of London, burned by Boudicca, bombed in the Blitz, the deadly nightshade bore its berries. The fruit spread and more and more nightshade sprouted round the city.

Maria Spiridonova had decided at an early age never to be the pawn of power. Her family had fought the Tsar, then the Bolsheviks. They knew what it was to constantly strive and to fight against might bigger than yourself. Maria realised from an early age that you cannot defeat a swell that grows from a million raindrops to a thousand streams, to a hundred rivers, to become a great wave on the sea of life.

But a wave can be predicted. The moon plots the tides. Maria planned to harness the forces around her, channel them where she could and ride them out where she couldn't. She embraced witchcraft as a means of doing so. Witches had been in her family stretching back as far as anyone knew, but was now just something laughed at by most of her blood. Maria, though, born and raised in Whitechapel, carried all that history within her. She saw that in London, 1980, she might be better off than she'd be in the wilds of Eastern Europe, but she was still poor, and life for those without full pockets would ever be a struggle. The justice of this world was blind to the likes of her. She would wield the sword and tip her own balance.

On a silver platter in front of her, still within the circle, was a white, wax doll some three or four inches in height. It was crudely shaped but most definitely a person, and one with some mug on 'em. Scrawled into the wax of the chest, in an approximation of a t-shirt, was the word Madness. The wax had been pressed into shape around a scrap of cloth holding blood and snot from a skinhead 'erbert called Larry. To one side of her was an open black-covered book, to the other a small athame.

A fortnight before Maria had been down the tube on her way for a drink with mates in Whitechapel when this same skinhead, Larry Hunt, had clocked her. He thought he was a Billy Big Bollocks but really was just an annoyance. He swaggered over and plonked himself in the seat next to hers. He tried to talk, but she'd just stared blankly at him. His drunken slurring hadn't made him any more attractive. The more she ignored him the more insistent he got. He leaned closer and closer to her, breathing stale beer, and then placed his hand on her thigh, running his hand up and down a few inches of the 501s she was in. She was insulted by this pathetic grope and decided to take revenge. She smiled coldly at him and ran her hand through his hair to take a few loose strands, but it was too closely cropped for that to work. He was partial to cheap billy, his nose ran more than Brendan Foster, she'd lifted a crispy kerchief from his 'arrington pocket as she got up for her stop. Sure enough, it was stiff with snot and spotted with blood.

This dark evening she'd pressed warm wax around a torn strip of the handkerchief and moulded it to shape, including a prominent prick. She went about her mystical work, muttering incantations while she rubbed cold water onto the phallus of the doll. Slowly the penis drooped and then smoothed away to nothing.

Not far across the East End, Larry Hunt was dry humping a sort. She was getting irate though, as for all the good talk he'd put up, nothing was getting put in. 'Sorry, babe, it's errr... it's just the beer. I'll be all right soon. This never happens. It's errr... errr... just the beer,' he stammered.

She pushed him off herself, melodramatically dusted herself down and flounced out of his bedsit without saying a word.

That very evening, the first 'Larry Hunt can't get it up' was written in the Ladies toilet in the Still and Star pub tucked just away from Aldgate tube in a street known as Blood Alley. Within a week, pencil leads were working hard, the message was scrawled in toilets and on walls across the East End and not just in the disgruntled girl's hand. Hunt had become a laughing stock. As the toaster popped up enthusiastically at the start of each day, he was reminded of the lustre he was lacking.

CHAPTER 2

Dalston: a less than salubrious manor on the fringe of east London. In the upstairs room of a pub, the Crown and Castle, Ingrid was dancing. Joe wasn't with his girlfriend, as he was out of town with the football. Even though the dance floor and bar were packed with youths, Ingrid was on her own. She was sporting red hipster trousers, low round her waist and with a white belt holding them up and highlighting her hips. The hem of her trouser legs sat above the ankle and on the outside leg an inch-long inverted V had been cut and tailored. Topping this was a blue and white striped matelot shirt. Her feet were in navy-blue canvas deck shoes with a white sole and sharply tied white laces. 'Very nautical,' Joe had said when she'd bought them down Blackman's off Brick Lane. The whole outfit had already been in her head when she'd got them. Right now her feet were sliding forward and back as a Purple Hearts record was getting the place dancing. Millions like us, oh yes there's... She looked good and felt good knowing it.

Ingrid wasn't dancing for show, in this moment of the weekend she'd built a space of her own.

The music spoke to her, more than street-corner politicos ever could, and being an individual in this small crowd of smartly dressed kids her own age gave her a sense of belonging that the race and nation they barked about ever would. To be able to move the way she wanted, to rhythm she'd chosen, without men gawping at her, bosses bossing, fish fingers all in a line was like stepping through the door into a different kitchen.

Her focus was on the moment, on the music and on her movement. The sounds a springboard to her mood for the weekend. She was precisely dressed, the details setting her apart from the average.

*

Mick Dakin had already caused a bit of bovver before he'd even got to the Crown and Castle. A couple of young mod lads were waiting for traffic to stop at the crossroads of Kingsland Road and the Balls Pond Road. They were in overly new Sta-Prest and pristine parkas that had the obligatory Jam and Secret Affair patches sewn onto them. Not that stylish, but they were only pishers. Dakin had got on the 38 bus at Islington's Packington Estate and got off at the Balls Pond Road stop when he'd eyeballed the two lads. The pub was just the other side of the road, but Dakin stomped up behind them, thumbs in the belt loops of his 501s, making sure his Doc Martens made as loud a stomp as possible. They were waiting to cross when he loomed over between the pair of them. They were barely, if at all, out of school and Dakin's couple of years of age on them gave him a good six inches of height over them. To the couple of frightened lads he looked bigger. In slow-motion Status Quo dancing he nudged first one with his elbow, and then with his other, the remaining lad.

'You're not going to the Crown, are you, lads?' he asked in a suggestive tone.

Not sure if it was a genuine question or a cue to a slap, it could go either way with skinheads, one lad answered, 'We might do, thought we'd get a beigel first.'

Dakin chuckled. He knew, as did the lads, that the beigel shop was in the opposite direction, only five minutes away and across the road on Ridley Road market.

'I'd do that if *I* were you,' he sneered.

The youngsters took the hint, changed direction and walked away from the pub towards Ridley Road.

Dakin chuckled. He was a bully. One of those arseholes who think they're tall because they've cut down everything around them. One of the things he used to swell himself up with was that he was mates with Kessler, Kessler, the skinhead who'd been jailed for life for a string of vicious killings the previous year. Kessler was now sat in prison

11

caught between puzzling how he'd been jailed for the werewolf murders he'd not done and enjoying the notoriety of being a known killer.

The fact was Dakin had only met Kessler a couple of times, at the bar at gigs at that. They'd had a pint or two, but in the company of a dozen or so other lads. The way Dakin used this loose connection was to plug himself into the juice of Kessler's reputation. The world didn't value who he was, where he was from and such brains as he had, so Dakin focused on his physicality, in particular his fists. He drew attention to them with prominent tattoos on his forearm. The left had a dagger and scroll, 'Arsenal' written boldly inside, the right a seated pig getting a nosh which was copied from the Pork Dukes' single 'Bend and Flush'. Very punk rock. These drew the eye, then a stick man 'Saint' figure in the pinch of flesh between thumb and index fingers. This from a tattooist called Saint on Portobello Road who'd give a discount if he could also put a saint figure on you. The predictable LOVE and HATE across his knuckles were left to tell the rest of the very short story.

Walking into the upstairs of the Crown, the first thing he did was clock who was there. Being a bully, he wanted to make sure he was the biggest thing there. If he wasn't he'd toady accordingly to whoever was the biggest lump.

The next thing he did was sweep the room for

people to pick on, girls to pick up. Just as he fell in step with the biggest muscles in any room, so he expected others to, women especially. His eyes peered round the room, noticed Ingrid, feeling secure in his brawn he regarded her with more prurient interest. She was a looker all right, and on her own, so it seemed at least. She was in the heart of the dance floor. To get there Dakin would have to dance. He could do that monkey arms swinging move that all the skinheads that can't dance do and jump about to punk, but dancing was a confidence and self-awareness he didn't have. He knew he'd look a lummox if he hit on her now.

Dakin decided to position himself at the bar, keep an eye on her and wait for her to come for a drink or edge in on her if she moved to the door or the toilets.

Maria was also in the pub and stood with her back to the bar watching the dancers. Her foot was tapping to a sixties song, 'Mony Mony', given a mod revival by sarf London girls the Spiders. A witch she might be, but that didn't mean she was a nebbische. She liked a dance, a drink, and to look crisp as much as every other east London teenager did. Tonight she was in a 'Fiery Jack' t-shirt, yellow miniskirt and black canvas Converse basketball boots. Her black hair was a shaggy bob, messy but styled so. It hung low over her eyes, made them difficult to see but she could regard all.

She watched Dakin snaking his way through the people pressed at the bar as Ingrid also made her way to it, Dakin's eyes on her. As Ingrid reached the bar, in a small gap next to Maria, he looked her up and down appreciatively. He put his fingers on her forearm as it rested on the bar with money for her lager and lime in hand and was about to start his routine when Maria swung her legs round, pulling Ingrid closer to her and making her legs a barrier between the skinhead and the girl. Dakin was a bit taken aback but looked Maria up and down appreciatively and said, 'There's only one thing better than a bit of leg...'

There'd been a time her heart would have dropped at so pathetic a come-on, but now she'd the confidence of flexing some power, her heart hardened. Maria asked, 'What?'

'A lot', Dakin returned.

She made as if she couldn't hear and leaned a little bit closer, smiling but with a quizzical expression. Ingrid also looked puzzled.

Dakin leaned in to repeat his remark and as he did so Maria's hand slightly tipped the base of his beer glass, sending beer running from it and splashing onto his jeans.

He was torn between saving face or his beer. Maria laughed and grabbing Ingrid's hand, they both skipped off and were lost in the mess of movers in the middle of the room.

'Faaaark,' Dakin cursed, the damp patch spreading across his crotch, but they were gone. He just caught sight of them at the opposite end of the pub heading for the door. Maria even had the cheek to lift her leg in a saucy music-hall back kick as she made the top of the stairs.

CHAPTER 3

The day was what the Stranglers would call 'sicky yellow'. Not a radiant and healthy yellow, the sort best flushed away. The tube train was rattling its way through suburbs to the greenery on the fringe of east London. The trees of Epping Forest dug deep into ancient earth, the ground covered in leaves turning to mulch, the sun was dying lower and lower through their branches. As Joe watched through the window he saw a hawk stoop and rise from the grass with a leveret in its claws.

Joe tensed. He knew that every full moon he too became a predator, a beast. He wasn't sure how or why, but he had no dispute about what. When the moon was due to brim he tried to get distance between himself and people, especially the people he loved. In the old werewolf films, the cursed would lock themselves away when the moon reached its climax. The thing is there ain't too many attics nor basements in east London you could chain yourself to of a night. Not unless you had the money and were into that sort of thing.

Joe got off the tube at North Weald, one of those weird stations that is countryside rather than

London, and started to walk as the sky dusked. The forest still had some wilderness. The deer at Clissold Park had no chance, but so much death in so small an area just brought attention, there's only so much east London considers 'normal'. The forest had deer, badgers, rabbits. Joe hoped their blood could sate the savagery within him. As the horns of the deer rise to glory, so the beetle and worm creep to earth.

*

Crabs, given the moniker cos his real name was Guy Smith, had been to interview the band Crass for his zine, *Permanent Smile*. It was becoming obligatory over the last year for every punk fanzine to have a Crass interview, and the band had a lot to say. They made a distinct musical noise: tinny bass, heavily fuzzed guitar and a yelled polemic. The lad didn't want his zine to be the only one without.

As with many a middle-class dropout, the band spat on the world they lived in, said people should think for themselves and then spent a lot of time telling them how they should. These beatnik pacifists posing as punkniks knew enough about fashion to use a cockney-voiced young oik to belt out the words. Those with the luxury of dropping out so often spend their time telling those that society never let in all about it.

They promoted anarchy. Joe's family had been Bundists and Anarchists in the East End at the start of the 1900s, and earlier back to Eastern Europe against the Tsar. The hands-on anarchism of the print and sweatshop workers was one where people collectively fought against bosses rather than just dropped out. Having seen some of the punks and being told that anarchy was in fashion, Joe's granddad quipped that even during the Spanish Civil War the CNT had found soap and water. Joe's great-grandparents had read Rudolf Rocker's anarchist newspaper *Arbeter Fraint*, Workers' Friend, and gone to meetings at the Sugar Loaf pub on Hanbury Street, where the anarchists and reds met, debated and organised.

In 1885, the anarchist Lucy Parsons had said: 'Let us devastate the avenues where the wealthy live'; in the 1920s she was described as 'more dangerous than a thousand rioters' by the Chicago Police Department. No guitars, no punk rock, no logo... just a small, black woman, way more direct than Crass were, speaking up and amplifying the rage of the downtrodden.

Crabs wasn't exactly raging, he'd interviewed Crass at their nearby commune, Dial House, and was now drunkenly asleep. He'd brought a few bottles of cider but it turned out the band preferred cups of tea, served in good china, too. Not what he'd expected but they'd been pleasant and answered all of his questions. He'd recorded the interview on a cassette and scribbled down a few notes as well. All of these were stuffed into his army surplus shoulder bag. There had been a couple of bottles of Merrydown in there but he'd started to drink these walking back from Dial House to the bus stop. It was evening and he wasn't sure if buses came this way; he could walk to the tube but the drink was making itself felt. At first he'd swaggered along the side of the road bellowing Crass' song 'Do They Owe Us A Living'. For many a punk Crass' dropout anarchism was a lazy justification to drink cider, shout 'smash the system', and idleness. For Joe's grandparents the idea of no police and no bosses had made them more disciplined, not less.

North Weald tube was a commuter station and, helpfully, only open for peak hours. Crabs would have to get a bus over to Epping, a bit of a journey, and then the tube to town. He still had his cider so he wouldn't be alone. As the second bottle started to spread its glow Crabs felt drowsy. He lay on the grassy verge by the bus stop, just for a moment, but soon drifted off into drunken slumber. His bag made a pillow and he was laid out like a stone medieval knight on a tomb, albeit a scruffy one.

It was the sharp snap of a branch that woke him, then the brushing of something through the twigs and leaves. He opened an eye, peered this way, then that, but saw nothing. He closed his eye and tried to drift off again, but then the crack of another twig jerked him fully to consciousness. It was coming from behind him, away from the road, and over his left shoulder. He stood up to see what it was. Dusk had fallen but he could still see as far as the bushes beyond the verge. The brambles and hazel were definitely moving, badger maybe? No, the movement was too high up. Then, suddenly, a pair of bright yellow eyes pierced the twilight. As his locked with them all movement froze, the evening fell silent. The brush of bushes had ceased and birdsong died.

After a moment that seemed a prog rock album, a figure stepped forward. The branches caught on the body, brambles snagged. Slowed slightly but relentless, whoever, or whatever, it was pressed doggedly forward.

The punk was still slightly unsteady on his feet, he was still woozy from the nap and two bottles of strong cider, but his head was clearing quickly and the rosy glow of his drunk was fading as the cold clarity of the threat now facing him was asserted. He could feel his bowels loosen, fear or drink he wasn't sure.

Slightly hunched but keeping the bright yellow eyes boring into his, Crabs could see it was someone in Dr Marten boots, jeans, a black and white 'Down in the Tube Station at Midnight' t-shirt, and an open black 'arrington. This someone was more a something, a distant echo. The face was furred, eyes shone fiercely from the snarling visage. The hands were curled and clawed. As the figure started to move, slowly at first, towards him, the hands flexed in and out from the ball of a fist to spread fingers and pointed claws. Crabs wondered if the Crass sigil he'd painstakingly Airfix painted onto his black combat jacket had invoked some demon?

As the figure advanced, it was obviously becoming clearer and clearer it meant him no good, Crabs stood transfixed, his face so taut with fear three of his half-dozen spots burst. Though not a cold night he could see the breath of the creature as it exhaled from its twisted nose. It was close now and Crabs could even smell it. Above the stink of his clothes, below the tang of his cider, there was musk. Breathing it in deeper he realised it was more of a must, like that of porn found in a carrier bag under a hedge.

Just then Crabs' funk burst, the beast was too close for him to run: it would be on him as soon as he turned. He reached down and picked up the cider bottle he'd been drinking from. He grasped the neck in his hand, a hand sweaty with cold fear. He swung once, twice, but the beast paused, leaned slightly back, and the bottle arced harmlessly. Crabs kept swinging, shouting, 'Fuck off! Fuck off!' repeatedly. The bottle landed on the beast's arm, but the limb was covered in coarse hair, the skin was as leather and the bottle bounced back without shattering. The force of the recoil swung Crabs' arm out and back. At the full extent, with the bottle in hand extending his arm and opening him up, the creature lunged. Claws raked Crabs' face, shreds of pimpled skin fell to the ground, cuts of flesh plopped to the floor and pus rose through the gore. Blood poured thick, time ran thin.

Joe was on the first tube back from Epping to London. He'd woken in the forest, next to a muddy puddle. His clothes were a mess; knowing it to be a full moon he'd worn old gear. He washed his face as best he could in the accusing reflection of the puddle and got some of the drek from his jacket and jeans. At least on a train coming back from Essex covered in filth such people as were about would just take you for a Crass fan. They might have a feeding of the 5000... but the wolf has to eat, too.

CHAPTER 4

Joe was noshing a plate of tzimmas. Next to it sat a slice of apple strudel. Both were hot and hearty, just what he needed.

After getting home from Epping he'd changed and then put his clothes straight in early to the laundrette. Apart from the old woman in the blue housecoat doling out washing powder and mopping the floor, he'd been the only one there. He didn't look at the state his clothes were in. He didn't like to think about the night before and never remembered what had happened, a blessing to a curse. He'd thrown them from the holdall he used to use for school into the drum and the suds and cycles of the machine beat yesterday from the wash. The chemical smell of wet washing powder cleared his nose and his head. The clock ticked forward, traffic started to build on Stoke Newington Church Street and the city came to life.

Once he'd taken the dried and folded laundry home and put it into his bedsit's knackered wardrobe, shirt and trousers hung, underwear shelved, he had a short nap and then went to meet Mark Hazell in a local caff. Mark was more Ingrid's friend, but he had a feel for the supernatural, and a bit of a gift with it. He'd felt instinctively there was something not right with Joe and had known that it was the wolf. He also knew that there was goodness in Joe. He'd told Joe that something could be done about it if it was done soon.

They'd arranged the meet a few days ago at Mark's suggestion, and the appointment was written on the cover of a *Kill Your Pet Puppy* zine lying by Joe's bed, great name and ubiquitous Crass screed. Strangely, Mark had said they should meet the day after the coming full moon.

Joe didn't know it, but Mark had deliberately suggested meeting as the moon started to wane as he wanted Joe to have the sense of regret he'd have after the transformation. Mark wanted that qualm to edge Joe to a difficult, but better, change.

Now he was sat in the caff deep into the sweet carrot stew. The morning after a full moon he never felt like eating meat, a feeling that always made him a little anxious. He also worried that Mark was taking his time. Joe was hoping to get down to M&D Records on Dalston Lane. There was a Greensleeves 12 tearing dances up, Johnny Osbourne's 'Fally Ranking', and Joe was itching for a copy to drop at home. Werewolf he might be, but he'd also a skinhead's thirst for reggae music. He hoped Mark wouldn't be much longer.

He wasn't, but neither was he alone. He came through the door of the caff accompanied by a sharply dressed mod girl. There shouldn't be any other type of mod, but sadly, just as hairs from a precise geometric loosely clog the plughole, there are. She was resplendent in a red Fred Perry V-neck over a buttoned-up white Fred Perry shirt that had blue and red striped trim on the collar. A fine-link silver chain hung down from beneath the collar of the Perry. There was what looked like some sort of star hanging from it, but it was slightly hidden by the jumper, Joe couldn't clearly see what it was. Her shaggy raven pixie cut feathered to the turn of the collar at the back of her neck. Looking down Joe saw she was also sporting crisply pressed trousers with a black and white dogtooth fleck, cut to a tight hem. Her purposeful walk caught the eye and made a statement as much as the directness of her movement, the sharpness of her look. Red socks echoed the scarlet of her jumper, and black basket-weave K Skips completed her careful silhouette. She was quite the sort.

Joe was surprised, not only because she wasn't due to be here, but as he'd not expected Mark to be with a girl, no matter how sharp. He had girl friends, but not a girlfriend, his attractions didn't pump it up that way.

Mark pulled out a chair, indicating that the girl should take it and then sat down opposite Joe.

'This is Maria,' he introduced, 'and this,' he said, gesturing with his hand, 'is Joe.'

Joe looked at them both, a bit puzzled as to why she was there. He was working his tongue around a raisin from the tzimmas that had got stuck in his teeth and was feeling the awkwardness of this first impression on such a good-looking girl.

She regarded him. Her face was hard to read. She didn't look friendly, but she didn't look unapproachable either. Joe put down his fork and leaned back on his chair.

'Maria is a mate of Ingrid's,' Mark continued. Since they'd left Dakin looking a chump in Dalston she and Ingrid had been out a few times. Mark had first met Maria with Ingrid down Petticoat Lane and knew straight away she was gifted like himself, but in a much more powerful way. Maria had picked up on this connection between them, too, but not mentioned it to Ingrid. Instead, she and Mark had met privately in a pub and talked. That conversation had led to this meeting.

Mark's voice dropped to a whisper, 'Maria's a witch.'

Joe was taken aback. He couldn't work out if Mark was joking. If he was, he didn't think it was a very funny joke.

'A witch?' Joe questioned.

Maria leaned close to him and speaking low but steadily and clearly said: 'If werewolves are real then hobgoblins and witches must be, too. You can see hobgoblins outside of a pub any night of the week, as for witches...'

Apart from himself and Mark no one knew about the werewolf. Joe's world suddenly dropped, he felt as though he was plummeting, and broke into a sweat.

'Don't worry, she can help,' Mark reassured. 'Really.'

'Joe, I can,' she threw out. 'You do want to be helped, don't you? Is that something you want? You can put an end to what you're living through.'

Despite the maw that opened up under him, that sliver of hope was something wholeheartedly wanted and grasped at. But what did she mean by 'end'?

'What... what would I have to do?' Joe asked. He didn't think it would be anything easy.

'You,' said Maria, 'don't have to do anything.'

Mark tapped the table top positively.

'Somebody has to take this curse from you. Somebody has to want everything you've got and they have to take all of it from you.'

'Everything, Joe, they've got to want all you love.'

Joe had a hundred questions at once all wanting to tumble out. He was also stuck with how bizarre this conversation was for a small Stamford Hill eatery. It was a little past noon, as far from night as could be, and the sun was reflecting from passing cars and shining through the large windows. He was sat at a Formica-topped table, with an HP bottle on it, while a kelnershe, a waitress in this kosher caff, bustled through with plates of food in each hand. Joe was about to speak when she approached the table to take orders from the two new arrivals. She smoothed her pinny and pulled a small notebook and pencil from the pocket.

'Three teas, please,' he ordered without thinking.

'We can lift this from you, Joe,' Maria said hopefully.

'We?' Joe asked. Did she mean Mark?

'It will take more than I can do on my own,' Maria started to explain. 'I am not the only witch, there are more of us. All of us can probably do it, and you have to work with us...'

Joe nodded.

'... and it must be secret.'

'Ingrid doesn't know about this part of my life, just as she doesn't know about yours. It will have to stay that way for now.'

They talked more and then went their separate ways. She'd told Joe what he had to do next. Joe's head was spinning. Was she serious? Could she do this? Who was she? Could this horror end?

Three empty mugs were left. This caff was good enough to be passed by the rabbinical court, the Beth Din, but it was still Stamford Hill, Hackney, east London. The ketchup was in a plastic tomato-shaped bottle on the table. The strudel sat uneaten and the spice from it permeated the room.

His hands were deep in his pockets, he was lost in thought as he walked down the broad expanse of

Stamford Hill towards his bedsit on Cazenove Road at the foot of the street.

Witches? Could they be real? Well, she was right enough about werewolves. He knew for sure that they existed in this world. She wasn't wrong about hobgoblins either. Over the last few years he'd seen loads of bands in the Rochester Castle: The Jam, Cock Sparrer (before they'd been banned), Black Slate... punk, reggae, pub bands. He'd been drunk, been in the fights, been part of the fun. He'd seen the hobgoblins tumbling out of the door at closing time, all mess, bile and aggression, and been one of them.

CHAPTER 5

Ingrid and Joe were snuggled in Joe's bed. It was Saturday morning and, as usual, the sound of chanting and praying murmured through from the yeshiva just next door. The road outside is a favoured shortcut for cabbies, and the rattle of sherberts was starting to pick up already. All day chassidim would be walking briskly into the yeshiva, peyess flying, their books clutched tightly to their chest. The road was at the heart of what is sometimes called 'the square mile of piety', and the numerous chassids in their distinctive black satin overcoats and shtraimlech, for shabbes, bustling back and forth showed the manor had well earned that reputation. As well as this fervent religious study, the Kray twins had also lived on the street. Joe's mother frequently remarked 'ugly people are the proof of G-d'. At the far end of the road from Joe, the twins had flats, one above the other, in a small, modern 1960s block. One of the most famous photographs of the twins is them striding out from the flats. None of their many chassidic neighbours can be seen.

Local gossip had it that Ronnie's flat had been used for romanticised orgies worthy of Heliogabalus.

Whatever the truth of that, Ingrid was doing her best to get something started with Joe. He was still asleep but was demonstrating he was full of life. The first mitzvah in the Torah is 'to be fruitful and multiply'. Ingrid wasn't Jewish and was on the pill but both young people had been practising their multiplication tables vigorously over the past year.

Under his leopard-spot duvet, he thought manly, she thought Jackie Collins, Ingrid snuggled closer and Joe started to stir, he opened one eye and then the other and gave her a smile. He liked to start the day by putting an album on and making coffee. Through one bleary eye over Ingrid's shoulder he could see the sleeve of the Ranking Slackness album stood against his bookcase. He'd hoped to be listening to 'Fally Ranking' but he'd still not got the chance to get a copy. Ingrid already had other ideas and as Joe rose slightly she pushed him back and then swung herself on top of him.

'No coffee?' he queried, but not complained.

'I'll give you strong and hot,' chuckled Ingrid. She was astride him and as she settled back her breasts were brushing his face. Joe was thinking that boobs are a question to which there is no wrong answer. He kissed one demanding nipple, and then the other. It's no wonder Madeline Smith in the framed photo on Joe's bookcase was so wide-eyed.

Where one was convex, the other concave, their congress a conversation where no one spoke too loudly and each listened. All too often sex is one person shouting their name into the void. All the void offers back is a diminishing echo.

Not too far away, as the crow flies, into the East End, Maria Spiridonova was also getting a start on the morning. She'd spent the previous evening at a Circles gig. She relished the aggressive punch they brought to their performance. The show had its share of posturing and posing but the band wound energy tighter and tighter until they cut loose and it burst free.

She was doing her best to ride that again now. She was astride a callow youth that she'd brought back to the small flat she shared with fellow witches Joanne Sulley and Susanne Catherall close to Brick Lane.

His Levi's, red Fred Perry, desert boots and underwear were scattered round the floor of her room. Her clothes from the night before were carefully folded on a chair, her suede jacket hanging from a wooden hanger on the front of her wardrobe, covering most of the full-length mirror that ran down its right-hand door. Hidden, her ceremonial robe was inside, tucked away to the left.

There'd been a smell on him from the night before. Not just the beer and sweat of a Friday night, but one of desperation. Not an edge he'd admit to but one that Maria was all too aware of in most of the lads she met. She saw right through the swagger of statement badges, tattoos and Brut to the insecurity all of those were there to hide.

This lad had lust running through him like the blue in Stilton. Without even knowing it he'd done exactly as he was told. He was lying on his back with Maria's knees gripping him. She had one arm reaching back with his marble bag in her fist.

'Say...' yank, 'my...' yank, 'name.' Twist, she was barking into his eye-popping and reddening face.

What made this so much fun for her was that she was well aware he had no idea of what her name was. Last night's lager had seen to that. He was now fully conscious that he wasn't in control of what was happening, and Maria was savouring his rising fear.

Every one of her yanks drew a sharp breath from him, but the twists caused him to yell and to buck, driving him deeper into her. There was no choice in his thrusting; all that was down to her and to when and how far she twisted. The control she had over her own pleasure excited her more than the taut dick.

Maria's family was Russian. Her grandfather had fled. He'd fought the Tsar, and then as a Left SR, escaped the Bolsheviks who were jailing and killing all the other revolutionary groups as they bureaucratised the Soviets.

In 1907 Stalin stayed at Tower House on Fieldgate Street in Whitechapel. Jack London stayed at the same place earlier, in 1902, and in his *People of the*

Abyss said it was packed with 'life that is degrading and unwholesome'.

Maria wanted none of the poverty she'd grown up in. She'd not forgotten the splinters she got in her hands as a child from collecting fruit boxes at Spitalfields Market and stamping them down for firewood to keep the family warm. She dressed well but not high-street fashions. She liked that working-class kids in east London styled as mods and skinheads. They showed they were a cut above the bosses and students who looked down on them. That presentation of self was a glamour, as was how she used her looks when she chose to.

What is often passed off as magic is frequently psychology. Manipulation is often a matter of knowing who a person is, the situations they'll get themselves in, being aware of how they'll react, and then the repercussions that will follow. It's no prophecy, nor sorcery, but can be played as such. Move the hands of a clock to the wrong time and that room will unsettle, Maria knew that, and had studied people, as well as plants like belladonna, and their chemistry. Maria also believed in a real power running through people and places, too. She could create magic. Too often the magic used by her fellow witches was petty, wasted on office politics and romance. It was small-change vengeance where they'd write a name on and burn a photo, much as a writer might ridicule the manager who'd made them redundant by having them killed off in a story.

Maria knew there was more, wanted more: to live deliciously. She could be a lift to her friends and a scourge to her enemies. She felt the excitement in dance, and lust, and in the panic of the lad beneath her.

She was still demanding he say her name, yanking his bollocks, and knew full well he didn't have a Scooby what her name was.

As her pleasure peaked, she leaned forward and whispered into his ear, 'It's Joanne.'

Her hand now pressed down on his chest as he came vigorously shouting, 'Joanne! Joanne! Farkin' 'ell, Joanne!'

Maria got sauce to her pleasure knowing that Joanne in the next bedroom would hear the name being yelled in an orgasmic frenzy and wonder what on earth was going on.

Joanne did and was staring wide-eyed at Susanne who was sat on the bed next to her.

Once he was spent, once his usefulness to her was over, he dressed limply. Maria blew him an enthusiastic but obviously fake kiss and he stumbled down the narrow stairs to the front door. Reaching for the latch he noticed a small sign pinned above it: *Find 'em Fuck 'em Forget 'em*. It served as a comment on lads such as himself, as well as a statement. The week the three girls had moved in Maria had written it out, laughed and pinned it to the door.

Maria was already running a bath, brushing her hair and laying out clean clothes. Saturday morning, post was being thrust through the letterboxes of the nation. Giro cheques and bills: like an Irish publican at the cusp of the lock-in, Maggie gives and Maggie takes away.

CHAPTER 6

From Commercial Road the Limehouse Pyramid thrusts up like an occluded tooth in the churchyard of St Anne's, one of Hawksmoor's churches that supposedly form a five-pointed star. The day falling to twilight adds to the air of mystery. The structure is twice the size of a man and no one is quite sure why it's there. Was it supposed to be atop the church? Do the words *The wisdom of Solomon* it bears hold hidden meaning? The large, white stone has long drawn the curious, crazed, and cabalistic.

Limehouse has long been an other. It was London's first Chinatown and for Sherlock Holmes and Denis Nayland Smith home to a den of opium, prostitution and foreign. Sax Rohmer, the creator of Nayland Smith and his nemesis Fu Manchu, had no understanding of Chinese culture but decided to create the villainous Fu Manchu after he'd asked on a ouija board what would make his fortune and the word C-H-I-N-A-M-A-N was spelled out. Anna May Wong lives there in the 1929 film *Piccadilly*, a film about the very different Londons that still permeate the city.

There's a scrape of earth at the base of the pyramid, on the face with the inscription. The grass is usually flecked with candle wax and who knows what has been placed beneath it. The apex extends down to a broad reach, or focuses to the heavens, depending on your cosmology or bent. The very meaning of a pyramid is unknown.

It was here that Maria Spiridonova had told Joe and her girls to meet. Here a ritual was to take place. The nineteenth-century occultist Eliphas Levi, best known for his image of Baphomet, wrote: 'God is the only absolute postulatum of all science, the absolutely necessary hypothesis fundamental to all certainty, and this is how our ancient masters scientifically formulated this certain hypothesis of faith: Being is. In Being is life. Life manifests itself through movement. Movement is perpetuated by the balance of forces. Harmony is a result of the analogy of opposites. In Nature, there is immutable law and also indefinite progress. A perpetual change of form, the indestructibility of matter, these are what one finds on observing the physical world.'

With this knowledge Maria knew that Joe and the wolf needed to be balanced, to kill the wolf would be to destroy Joe. But she could hurry the movement of life, progress the form of the wolf and utilise the perpetual change of form.

Maria was stood forward, facing the inscribed face of the pyramid. Behind that, and still in front of her, ran the Commercial Road beyond the churchyard railings. Behind her stood Joanne and

Susanne, they were nervous, their eyes darted from the looming church to the pyramid, to Maria. Maria knew what she would unfold, well, what should unfold. The girls did not. They had been told to follow the instructions that would be given to them.

Nearing twilight, the moon was announcing itself. Maria had told Joe to meet them here. He also was worried. He carried the horror that a full moon would precipitate an awful change in himself. Maria had said that she knew this, was prepared for the danger and that he would have to meet whatever came if he was ever to be freed from the malison holding him.

Joe shuffled nearer; already his blood was starting to course. His scuffed Dr Marten shoes brushed the dry dirt of the churchyard. No point in ruining his best, he knew. He tugged at the collar of his Fred Perry, the hair at the back of his neck was already rising.

Maria called his name and in her outstretched arm she held a silver-bladed athame. She'd got this particular blade for this particular ritual. Again, she loudly spoke his full name, 'Joseph Bovshover', as his yellowing eyes met hers. She held the knife level to him and then moved it to point to a pentagram drawn out on the ground in salt. The white of it was prominent against the green of the grass and the falling light. She indicated for Joe to stand within it.

He stepped forward to do so, hunching further and further as he did. He was trying to hold back the wolf in him but his resolve, on what was a hopeless task, weakened as the light weakened and the moon grew radiant. Once within the heart of the pentagram he couldn't step out. The tension of himself and the emerging beast grew fiercer and spiralled, sweat broke out thickly and ran down his back, clinging to the coarsening hair.

Maria moved forward, whispering. Her voice rose and both Joanne and Susanne could hear an incantation in an arcane tongue. They'd both done childish rituals and magic, only half believing in them, but this was a step above, or below, and becoming frightening for them. Maria called them closer. From the floor she picked up a sprig of wolfsbane, tied with scarlet thread, and gave it to Susanne. Joanne was given berried bryony tied with white ribbon. With the knife she pointed that they should stand at the bottom points of the pentagram. She remained between them and directly in front of the transforming Joe.

'Whatever happens, neither of you move,' she said firmly, then stressed, 'Do NOT move.'

Both girls felt cold, and it wasn't just the night. They were frightened. Maria's intensity and direction kept them together. They were both in short skirts and Italian-knit tops. Both had a hooded ceremonial robe loosely around themselves. They pulled these tighter for warmth and, increasingly, security.

Still reciting, Maria reached to her feet and picked up a ball of red yarn. Without breaking flow, she arced loop after loop over Joe. His eyes had yellowed, not to pallid sickness, but a shining fury. The crop on his head had grown thick and his once precise sideburns now covered the sides of his face. Drool hung from his mouth, more particularly from the sharp teeth that he bared as he grimaced at the threesome.

Maria wound a final round of wool around Joe. The yarn obviously would not hold him, but this was not the point of it. The beast in Joe had to tear free, and in doing so symbolically loose itself from the better part of Joe. This would not be the cure, but it was the first step in one.

With a sharp tug Maria yanked at the yarn, pulling it tight around the slavering Joe. At first the woollen thread bit into the muscles of Joe's arms, but as he grew stronger they grew tauter and tauter until the inevitable happened: the wool gave and snapped.

'Do NOT move!' Maria shouted. It was pointless to tell the beast this, but Joanne and Susanne needed the instruction. The now free arms of the wolf swung wildly at Maria, slashing left and right. She advanced cautiously but directly, with the knife held point forward. The beast rose to its full height; the moon now radiated brightly above the pyramid and the beast's fangs shone. Maria took another step forward; as she did so the wolf lunged. Maria was prepared for, and expecting, this. She slashed with the knife, a downward cut that caught the beast across the bridge of its snarling nose. The beast gave a start and stopped momentarily. A cut opened on its face and blood began to trickle.

Maria slashed again and again; downwards, upwards, left and right. Some sliced and some went wild, but those that struck home opened the beast's face and arms and blood flowed. The beast, unused to pain being inflicted, howled, turned and ran.

This was why the knife had a silver blade. This could injure the animal. At first it ran towards the railings and the Commercial Road, but seeing the iron spikes baring its way it turned and looped around the far side of the church and down towards the Thames.

Before it had a chance to swing fully around the church building Maria called the girls to her. 'Quickly, let's get out of here. *That* could be back any second!' As they ran towards the main road Maria wrapped the bloody knife in a piece of scarlet satin she pulled from her pocket. She'd brought it just for this.

The blood was vital, it was the point of this ritual. Now the three of them needed to get away quickly before they shed any of theirs.

The blade of the knife, now smeared in the wolf's blood, would be melted down, blood and all, and moulded into a pentacle, the symbol of the werewolf. A silver bullet can destroy the werewolf, its purity stop the unclean heart. Joe's blood mixed with the metal made this amulet specific to him. It would not stop the beast, or cure him of this curse, but now the werewolf and the amulet were linked.

Should someone want all that Joe had, want it and take it, put their hand on the amulet and take it from Joe, then all, including the hex, would pass to them.

CHAPTER 7

Joe felt as though he'd been through the wringer. Twice. From his bed he looked over at the scatter of clothes on his floor. They'd seen better days, too. His 501s were crumpled, he could clock blood spattered up their legs. His black Fred Perry showed less, but it sat awkwardly from stiffened, dried stains.

He ran his hand over his cropped barnet and got inelegantly out of bed. He stepped over the soiled clothes, and then turned and kicked them to the corner of the room towards a wicker wash basket. He walked over to his stereo and from the tumble of records leaned against the side of his bookcase lifted the first 12 he came to; Barrington Levy's 'Look Youthman'. Unusually for a reggae record it was pressed on green vinyl, like a lot of the punk records of the past few years. Dancehall reggae had boomed up the last year and this was a straight killer, so he slid the disc from the familiar Greensleeves sleeve and put it over the spindle of his record player, letting it plop to the deck and then hitting 45 and lifting the arm and the needle to the track. Choon.

With music and the Bialetti on the go he felt

better. The familiar ritual of making coffee in the moka was reassuring. He remembered there'd been something important with Maria yesterday; he wasn't sure what, but he knew why there was a blank. He now knew he wasn't blacking out from the drink at least.

He remembered a couple of other things, the bright yellow Greensleeves label rotating on the stereo reminded him that he'd still not picked up 'Fally Ranking', also that he had an arrangement to meet Maria, he had better shmatta put by for that. Mentally he calculated the lunar cycle – he was getting far too good at that – and he noted that it wouldn't be a full moon. Maria was trying to help, he knew that; this afternoon she was going to tell him what he needed to do next.

*

Maria had arranged to meet Joe at the bar just outside the ticket barrier but before the street, at Farringdon tube. She'd come down from Aldgate East and he could walk the short distance from where he worked at the printers in Clerkenwell. The bar had recently been spruced up. It was tiny, but popular with commuters, bummarees and dippers. The snob screens meant you could just about have a private conversation. The noise of passing trains frequently drowned out bonhomie. The stained glass inside was unusual and gave it a very different atmosphere from the grey of the tube tunnels. There were bars at several Metropolitan Line stations, as with most fancy things most were to the west of the City. Baker Street had a particularly welcome one where you could get off a train, have a beer and then continue on. Handy if you were off to the wilds of Ladbroke Grove, Hammersmith, or Wembley. Betjemen had a poem, 'The Metropolitan Railway', in his 1954 collection *A Few Late Chrysanthemums* that waxes lyrical about a smell of dinner and a pot of tea.

At not long after 5.30 p.m. the bar was still early doors but was getting full of people stopping 'for a quick half' on the way home from work. It wasn't Friday so the 'poets' day crowd, piss of early tomorrow's Saturday, weren't making a start on the weekend. By scowling she managed to get a seat inside. What she and Joe had to discuss was important and so she was confident he'd look for and find her among the growing press.

She wasn't there long when Joe walked in. He looked drained, and given the events of the previous night, a shift on the print, and all the weight on his shoulders, that wasn't surprising. There were cuts across his nose and cheek. Cuts that were already healing and looked a week or so old, Maria knew, though, that she'd slashed them just the night before.

He gave her a tepid smile and pointed to the bar. She gave him a thumbs up and lifted her bottle of

Double Diamond to indicate she'd have another. She hoped they'd both work wonders.

There was space at the bar but as punters clocked the moody skinhead with Mars bars across his boat more quickly opened. Joe looked over to Maria. She was smartly turned out as ever: beige jacket, powder-blue skirt, white ankle socks, and gleaming red shoes, an un-ruby Dorothy, Joe thought. With beers in hand, he came to join her, sitting heavily and letting out a long drawn-out breath. Maria leaned forward and smiled reassuringly.

'It's not that bad, Joe.'

'Really?' he asked. Like her he'd seen that night's *Stannerd* headlines and the paper sellers yelling ''Orrible East End Murder!' The savaged body of a property developer had been found by the Thames in Limehouse.

'You've a way out now. It's close.'

Maria reached into the pocket of her suede jacket and pulled out a small piece of tightly folded scarlet satin. She placed it in front of her and made a small circle with it three times on the table to draw Joe's attention. She then unfolded it and Joe could see that there was a gleaming silver pentacle on a closely linked chain sat there.

Maria lifted the amulet and proffered it to Joe. He reached out and took it in his hand. As soon as it was sat in his palm, he gave a shudder. His palm itched, and not in a way as if he was coming into money, but in an altogether more sinister manner.

'You're to wear this, Joe,' Maria continued. 'This is the sign of the werewolf.'

Joe did not look convinced. 'It's one thing to wear a Magen David or maybe even a Hamsa, but this?' he asked.

'The knife that cut your face had a silver blade, and it's been melted down, along with your blood that was on it, to make this,' Maria told him. 'You must wear it. It holds the beast within it,' her voice dropped, 'as do you.'

Rubbing the marks on his face Joe was not sure if he trusted this reasoning, but having some faith in Maria, and mostly out of desperation, he opened the clasp of the chain and hung the symbol around his neck. The amulet dropped down beneath his Adam's apple and sat on his chest.

'That's it,' encouraged Maria. 'You can't cure this curse, but you can pass it,' she whispered. 'If someone wants what you have, all of it, and takes it. Takes all that you have and this,' she pointed to where the amulet was hanging, 'then they'll become the beast. You'll be free.

'If that doesn't happen then the time you savage those you love gets closer and closer. That's the true curse.'

'All I've really got is Ingrid...' Joe stated.

'Then you've got to be prepared to let her go, for now, or lose her for ever,' Maria firmly told him.

Joe took stock, weighed all she'd told him. He'd nothing to lose really. He knew that if he did nothing, he'd end up with nothing. Worse yet he'd end with loss.

Maria carried on talking but none of it sank in. He was focusing on what she'd already told him and working out how to do what he needed to. But do something, he knew, he must.

A quote from Charles Fort's *The Book of the Damned* drifted into his mind: 'Sometimes I'm a savage who has found something on the beach of his island. Sometimes I'm a deep-sea fish with a sore nose.'

*

Mick Dakin had an unproductive day, an unproductive life should truth be told. Evening was edging and he'd hardly been out of bed all day. He'd had a dump, a slash and made a Pot Noodle. He'd thought about frying an egg for a sandwich but even that seemed too much effort.

The only use he'd put his hands to had been on himself. Stretched out in bed he'd let himself drift into a reverie of Ingrid. He'd fancied both her and her mate as soon as he'd seen them the other night in Dalston. The one that'd tossed beer down him, she could fuck right off, he thought. That didn't stop him introducing her to his fantasies about

Ingrid, though. They were both sorts.

He pulled his sheets tighter around himself and then started to pull himself again. It was something he was adept at, practice makes perfect.

Dakin was weighing up if the stripes of the matelot shirt Ingrid had been wearing when he'd first set eyes on her made her tits look bigger, from there he was reminiscing about the pull of her white belt and how it had emphasised the curve of her hips. The fineries of silhouette and look weren't apparent to him, he was about the furtive glance and 'aving a butcher's. What she was saying about herself was irrelevant to him, he wouldn't hear it even when spoken.

Dakin's dreams were less about love, more about asserting himself on the world. Usually, the only way he did this was by dolloping himself onto a tissue. That was the apex of his efforts, but all the same he was aggrieved about not having more. Like most kids in London he didn't have much of anything, including chances, but wasn't his revenge on that success?

Youth has always been trying to assert itself upon the adult world, in the sixties he'd been born into they had the money to do so. Teens now had the same energy as ever, but the wealth was, once again, out of reach for most. For all his rebellious swagger and all the punk rock revenge anthems that he sang along to, his thought, humour, and boots all kicked down. It was easier to do that than challenge what really checked him, and easy and sleazy was Dakin all over.

CHAPTER 8

Joe enjoyed the getting ready for a night out as much as the night itself. The flat he lived in had a shower shared by the three others on his floor. Many of the old Victorian houses in London had been converted this way. Give the serving classes jobs and make 'em pay.

Thoroughly clean and with a towel wrapped around his modesty he quickly sprinted up the half-dozen dingy stairs and through his door. He'd had the Ranking Joe choon 'Drunken Master' in his head as he'd rubbed and scrubbed. He made for the stereo and after flipping through a stack of 7s on top of his bookcase, next to his framed Madeline Smith photo, oh Madeline, and found his copy. He hoped it'd be a foreshadow of the coming night. Friday night and out to see a band, have a dance and down a few, kicking off with a solid slice of Joe Gibbs, too: business.

He set that to safely spinning and dusted himself with a liberal handful of talc, Brut talc at that, savagery. Once confident there was enough to enhance his manliness he stepped into his underwear; happy that was snug he dashed a shake of talc in there, too, the last place he'd want to be savoury. He picked up the amulet from the mantelpiece, he would be wearing it like he'd been told to, but it didn't 'alf itch. Probably just wasn't used to the metal, or maybe the points of the pentacle were catching?

The single had played through and looking for a longer groove Joe selected another Joe Gibbs, this one a discomix so it'd run longer and give him more time to do a little dance as he dressed: the mighty Earth & Stone singing 'Ring Craft', dropping into 'Dreader Mafia', a weird and wonderful take on the same riddim from Snuffy and Wally. When reggae went strange, reggae went right.

The next, and very important, move was to select his shirt for the night. He eased open the door of his wardrobe and clocked the button-downs. Looking at them like Harold Shand does the gangsters hung from meat hooks in *The Long Good Friday*; all his, and all in his power. Nobber on the rail, chinker in the laundry basket. There were gingham checks, windowpane, Oxford. Brutus, Ben Sherman and a couple of Arnold Palmer he was particularly proud of. Ten years before skinhead had been the fashion and the old coats, shirts and whistles were there to be had at the second-hand shops and markets. You needed to charper for the bona shmatta, but something bold could still turn up if you were lucky.

2 Tone and mod were all the rage now, and the streets were raging all right, and cheap clothes

for the yoofs filled the obvious shops. They were cheap and looked cheap. Joe was Stamford Hill and knew enough shneyders to have some discernment and east London enough to know buying quality second-hand was better than new cheap. Many an altered suit looked an absolute rascal, while a cheap one was never more than drek.

Running his hand over the shoulders of the coat-hangered shirts Joe first considered a powder-blue gingham check but then remembered the blue socks that would go with it were in the wash. As every good skinhead knows, shirt, socks, pocket square should accentuate one another. Given that, he went for a short-sleeved white number with an assertive black and yellow windowpane check. The collar was three-fingered and rolled seductively. He'd balance that with lemon socks, a chocolate tank top, and red Frank Wright loafers. Trousers before batts, though, and he looked into the wardrobe, shirts to the left, kaffies to the right, and pulled out a crisply creased black pair. They'd balance the black of the windowpane and not overshadow the dicky dirt.

He moved the paperback he'd finished that morning from his bed, Peter Cave's bikers v suedeheads *Rogue Angels*, and laid his outfit on top of his leopard-spot duvet, then dressed. Funny, thought Joe, that none of those New English Library aggro pulp writers got the details right.

Pulp fiction was nothing new to the lower orders of the city. In his *Curiosities of London Life*, from 1853, Charles Manby Smith himself had noted that London's Sunday markets had 'all abundance of the blood-and-murder, ghost-and-goblin journals, embellished for the most part with melodramatic cuts, where what was wanting in truth of artistic delineation was plentifully made up in energy of action. It would seem that there is a charm in pistols, daggers, bludgeons, and deadly weapons of all sorts, with the assaults and assassinations they suggest, that is irresistible to the population of London. No matter how gross the ignorance or stupidity of a writer, so that he have but a deed of blood or violence to unfold: a murder is so delicious a morsel to the palates of a debased multitude, that it imparts a relish to the most intolerable dullness, and invests imbecility itself with the attributes of genius and talent.'

Sartorially complete, if a little spiritually empty, Joe took an eyeful of himself in his wardrobe mirror. He wasn't one for a Fonz-type 'heeey!' but he thought he looked good. A liberal splash of Brut aftershave and he was good all over.

*

Everyone was turned out proper. A small group was slowly building up at the Swan, the large pub opposite Clapton Common. It was a bit of a mums and dads boozer but was handy for the 253 bus stop that'd take Joe, Ingrid and their mates to Camden Town to see the Mo-Dettes play.

Hackney lad Dale Robertson was first through the door, giving it large in a new Madness t-shirt that screamed '*FUCK ART LET'S DANCE*', why not indeed? Ingrid's china Joyce came in next, all Siouxsie Sioux backcomb and spookily made-up eyes, then Dennis, as puckish as ever and soon there was near a dozen before it was time to jump on the bus in order to get to the gig in time for the support band.

There was already an air of excitement just walking inside the venue. It was the Mo-Dettes and teenage hormones were racing. The crowd was a mix of punks, rude boys, skinheads, mods... no trouble yet but there'd no doubt be some.

The support band turned out to be pedestrian, an art school four-piece in mod whistles, not cos that's what they liked but cos they thought the current fashion was a road to success. Sadly, the look was threadbare and everyone saw through it. 'Farkin' tickets' was Dale's verdict. After a perfunctory look most people just made their way back and congregated at the bar.

The Mo-Dettes were altogether more exciting. They played poppy punk songs that appealed to the ska fans and the moddy types, too. They were always a blaze of style: shocking pinks, shocking attitude, confidently sexy and with more than a hint of menace. The look was for themselves, and that resonated with the outside-edge young women in the audience. The music had punch, the lyrics bite. The band's singer Ramona had previously been with another all-female band, Kleenex. This Swiss band had an interesting single out with Rough Trade, the sort of off-kilter abstract punk that appealed to Mark. Her slight European accent added to the band's air of being something different. An unusual wit was as much a part of the band as girls, instruments, and songs.

Many of the crowd were sporting Mo-Dettes badges, most of these had fifties cartoons on and played with, and undercut, stereotypical male and cute girl roles. Ingrid had a powder-blue one on the lapel of her burgundy and navy-striped boating jacket. There was a surge forward as the band took the stage. She took Joe's hand and they moved to the periphery of the throng.

From their first song people were dancing and enjoying themselves. The songs were tight, not profound, but a good time and the actual doing of it can say a lot more than the likes of the dour sour glower of 'Oh Vienna'.

Ingrid had caught the eye of Dakin who was on the far side of the dance floor. He saw that she was with a small group of people, but that didn't bother him. She seemed to be leaning into a lad he knew as Joe Bovver, which did. Dakin had eyes on her for himself.

Seeing that Joe had turned and walked towards the bar, Dakin stepped forward and made a move towards Ingrid. As he reached her, he lifted his pint and then comedically covered his bollocks with his other hand. Looking her in the eye he then lowered his to his covered 'nads and said, 'I see your mate from last time's not here,' meaning Maria. 'Let's keep these dry, shall we?'

Ingrid's heart sank a bit, she thought he was an oaf, but this was a bit funny at least.

'Err, yeah. I think we can do that.'

She was a bit unsure what to say or do. She didn't smoke and so had nothing to do with her hands, she didn't have a drink in one either so she couldn't take a sip and avoid conversation. Joe had gone to the bar... Joe!

She had an awkward minute that seemed a lot longer. She then felt a nudge at her elbow and Joe was behind her with a couple of drinks in his hand. She could tell from how he gripped the glasses that he was tense.

'Yours,' said Joe giving her the Bacardi and Coke.

'Mine,' he stated, looking fiercely at Dakin and lifting his pint. The implication was clear. While Ingrid appreciated Joe standing up for her if she needed it, she didn't like the way he'd put that. She was more than capable of dealing with twats and would have liked him to let her do so.

As Joe was obviously with Ingrid, for now at least, and with several mates, Dakin decided discretion was the better part of valour. He took a half-step forward towards Joe, spat 'Wanker!' turned and lost himself in the mess of kids jumping up and down to 'Paint It Black'.

Joe blew the froth from the head of his pint. 'Fucking ice cream,' he muttered after Dakin.

CHAPTER 9

The dogs: after football the second biggest spectator sport in the country. To the middle classes that often comes as a surprise. The Hackney Wick Stadium was the borough's main sporting venue since the Orient had moved to Leyton in 1937. It wasn't just ye workers who arose from their slumber for the team. The Orient had some toff patronage, too. In 1921, on 30 April, the Prince of Wales, the future King Edward VIII, became the first royal to attend a football league match. They played Notts County and beat them 3-0. No saviour from on high delivers, no faith have we in prince or peer, but he turned out to be lucky that day.

The King came to thank the team for their patriotic example during the Great War. Forty-one members of the team joined up, all to the 17th Battalion Middlesex Regiment which became known as the Footballers' Battalion. The Orient were the first team to join up together and had the highest number of players join up than any other team.

Hackney Wick was home to both the dogs and the Hackney Hawks for speedway. Joe had seen the Hawks walk out to the exciting and familiar strains of 'The Magnificent Seven', but the speedway attracted too many grebos for Joe's liking. The dogs, though, that was a good night out.

When the Orient moved out of their stadium in Clapton to go to Leyton, greyhound racing had moved in. The stadium closed in 1974 but locally to Joe there were the Hackney Wick, Walthamstow, and over by Finsbury Park, Harringay tracks. In 1937 Harringay had twice raced cheetahs.

Joe liked a night at the dogs, and Ingrid quite enjoyed it, too. You get a decent pie and can have a drink. Joe made the joke about the country going to the dogs.

'Symbolic, innit?' Ingrid responded.

'Them greyhounds,' she continued, 'they stick a muzzle on their boats, tweak their nuts, stick 'em in a box and send 'em tearing after a decrepit toy rabbit. No wonder them poor dogs are highly strung.'

It got Joe to thinking about one of the best books about their part of the world; Alexander Baron's *The Lowlife*. Baron had lived on Foulden Road and wrote about it in the book as Ingram's Terrace. The residential road was a short walk from Joe's street, Cazenove Road, at the far end of Stoke Newington High Street past the old bill station, well known as London's worst, and opposite the Walford pub.

Joe's grandfather reckoned Baron's *From the City, From the Plough* to be the best book about the Second World War. Joe saw the irony in someone who'd fought the Nazis in Italy and Normandy coming back to Blighty and having to anglicise his name, from Bernstein to Baron, in order to get his work published. That book about the war came out in 1948. The jackboot needn't be so heavy to be felt.

The low concrete terrace looked over the track, on the far side a large blackboard the size of a house displayed the info for the race so punters could place their bets with the bookies who had their pitches lined up between the terrace and the track. A long grey cloud hanging over it seemed to catch the mood of all concerned.

Ingrid had placed her first two bets on the six dogs. The dogs were being walked to the traps and she asked Joe to put her bet for the next race on the half-dozen again.

'You sure?' queried Joe. 'What is it with Tom Mix? Lucky number?'

'It's their little jackets I like,' she replied. 'They're a bit 2 Tone, ain't they?' she related.

'Look! Look!' Ingrid was suddenly bouncing up and down excitedly. 'That one just winked at me. He's bound to win.'

Joe shook his head and looked down dispiritedly to his well-shined brogues. 'Blind in one eye, more like,' he muttered.

From the corner of his eye, he could see his jibe had caused Ingrid a bit of pain. It did him, too. He didn't want to, but Joe knew that he had to put some distance between her and himself. It really was the last thing he wanted to do but knew he had to. To end the curse he was under, and to see Ingrid safe, he had to dig this ditch between them. He reached to the pentacle hanging on the silver chain around his neck. He could physically feel the draw to the dark in it right now. He'd thrown some deliberate moods to create that negative space.

He'd give up his printing job tomorrow, good as it was. He'd think twice about it, but he'd let his records and shmatta go. The one thing he had he really treasured was Ingrid. Maria had been clear: someone else had to take everything from him, or he'd end up destroying it all. Even though it broke him, Ingrid meant too much to him to let that happen.

For her part, Ingrid had noticed some digs and sulkiness from Joe over the last week. She just put it down to him being a moody git. Everyone has their moments, but now it was becoming all too common. She knew that blokes didn't break up with girls. Men did that thing where they created atmospheres or absences until the girl did the breaking up. Men are like leaves in the autumn: they dry, crumble and fall away.

Right now, the dogs were haring out of the trap, and she turned Joe's recent behaviour around in her head as she disinterestedly watched her dog lose. She noted that it lost, though. Perhaps it was a sign?

*

One of the good things about working on the print was that it was shifts. Not so good when it was an early start, though the money was welcome. The loud roar of the machines would drown out everything from the outside, leaving Joe with his thoughts.

Today Joe was sat in a barber's chair by mid-afternoon. He had his hair cropped every month, a number two in the summer and a four in the winter. The quarter-inch was fine for hot weather and had an edge to it. The grades on a barber's clippers move up in eighths of an inch and the half-inch of a number four gives a bit of cover and actually looks a bit smarter when the cold starts to bite. None of that *Quadrophenia* nonsense about lacquer neither.

Some of the punks were now sporting completely shaved heads and too-high boots, but Joe thought the comedy skinheads should be left to Roy Kinnear and Dick Emery. 'Dad, I got it wrong again', as Emery's clown skinhead catchphrase went.

Joe had been coming to Gino's at the bottom of Stoke Newington Church Street for years. He'd had his barnet cut there since he was a kid. The shop had opened in 1965 and so was just a bit younger than Joe himself. Gino still cut hair there himself. He knew what he was at and could razor a precise tramline into a crop. Different parts of London had different partings cut so they could clock who was who in a barney. Joe's went from the point of the left temple two-thirds of the way back to the crown. He had a double crown which gave him one hell of a cowslick when his hair grew out. He absently pondered if it was there when he werewolfed?

He felt the clippers pressing down onto his skull and relaxed into the vibration. Before long the barber was moving his head to this angle and that so he could tidy and complete the cut.

A lot of the gumby skinheads had bought their own clippers and cut their own hair. Even if you saved a bit of money, your mate never got your hair to look the business and you ended up looking far too Ivan Denisovich for Joe's liking. We can't take no more of that, no no no no no no, no we can't take no more of that.

Joe was sat back in the chair, waiting for the barber to finish and then check the back of the cut in the small mirror held up that reflected into the large mirror in front of the chair that Joe was peering into. It was less the mirror and more himself he looked into.

He was starting to itch. He wasn't sure if it was the trimmings of hair or the pentacle against the thin thatch of his chest. Ingrid still weighed on him. He'd wanted to just tell her what was happening, all of it. But Maria had said not to. She'd been adamant about it. Everything had to be taken from him. If he told Ingrid, it would change nothing. He couldn't give the hex away, it had to be taken.

Above the mirror were several of the hairstyle model pictures that all barbers had. These were a bit weathered, and it made all the punters at Gino's laugh that one of them was a framed picture of the *Stingray* puppet Troy Tempest. In the TV series Troy's girlfriend was Marina, Joe remembered. She never said a word, not because she couldn't but because she was under a curse and if she did another would die. But even with that muteness, things worked out between her and Troy. They were just puppets, but stories can give hope.

CHAPTER 10

The thing that really leapt out to the copper was the contrast between the white of the kid's jeans and the dark splashes of red upon them. At first, he thought it was just some colourful mess that the punk kids were wearing these days. But as his eye moved up the supine body it was clear that it was blood, a lot of blood.

PC Deens had been in the force a half-dozen years and had seen as much as most constables, even a couple of dead bodies, but he'd never seen anything as sickening as this.

The kid's torso had been torn open. The stomach was like the soft underside of a chip shop pie with the mince all sliding out. The blood was starting to crust around the tears, viscera slopping onto the floor and in a mess of hell. The lad was in a t-shirt; it looked like it might have been white, with some band or other on it. It was so torn and bloodied Deens couldn't make out what it said and wouldn't have known the band even if he could make it out. The only punk he knew about was Debbie Harry, and that wasn't for her music.

The face had been savaged, too. It would be hard to identify who this was... had been. He had white hair. Judging from the clothes he looked a teenager, so it was probably dyed hair.

The body lay in a small Hoddeston side road, a modest grey and unloved commuter town on the fringes of London. Side road was too much for this thoroughfare. It was more a dog-shit alley, every town has one. There were the expected white dog droppings, the dogs round here gnawed bones, scrubby brambles and nettles, with the only signs of hope being the verdant shoots pushing through the tarmac path. Even they were weeds, and the council would soon put them down.

The person who'd found the body would be written up as a 'dog walker', but the dog was there to do its business. None of that added to the dignity of the dead kid.

As soon as Deens had arrived after a panicked 999 call had been received, he'd radioed in for the detectives. What he saw in the alley was beyond the realm of normal police business. It was out of the realm of normalcy by any standard.

As a way of showing their place in the pecking order the detectives took their time arriving at the scene. By now Detective Sergeant Jan Vink was looking over the body and carefully going through the kid's pockets trying to find out who he was. Vink's Dutch family and name led to the nickname Van der Valk in the force. What Barry Foster had in spark, Vink had in a leisurely manner and deep tone.

There wasn't much on the lad: a couple of quid, a ticket for a Madness gig the previous night in London. The kid must have been there, caught a late train and been on the way home. Vink prayed he wasn't the kid of anyone he knew. Once they had a name, they could ask at the Rye House Tavern and the Bell about him.

Close to the corpse, caught in low bramble, was a record cover and, close by, the disc. The detective worked both free from the briars with a biro. Vink could see from the cover that it was a Madness single: 'One Step Beyond', that was one way of putting it, he thought. Written across the cover was 'to Penguin from Kix'. The ticket stub was for Madness, these were likely to be linked. Penguin? Was that what the kid was called? How'd he get a name like that? He looked over to the kid's face to see if there was a prominent nose that gave reason for the name. There was no nose, just a ragged flap of flesh hanging over a gaping wound where a finger should have been picking.

The record itself had four deep scratches running across the grooves. It wasn't until the forensics were examining it that they noticed the innermost stopped close to the run-out groove by the label, right by the tiny etched words 'A PORKY PRIME CUT'.

*

The thing that really leapt out to Dakin was Ingrid's arse in white jeans. The things he could do to that. She'd been dancing for the last half-hour since arriving at the Mildmay Tavern on the Canonbury end of the Balls Pond Road. The pub was a mod stronghold and Dakin had deliberately gone for penny loafers along with his normal Ben Sherman and a bright red Fred Perry V-neck. Boots and braces wouldn't be appreciated at the Mildmay, but the smarter end of skinhead came from mod. Looking snappy got him through the door and gave him a chance with the girls there.

The boozer was a big Victorian building taking up a street corner, on the border of Islington and Hackney. The main entrance for the brick-red pub was on the Balls Pond Road, and just around the corner was the door to the saloon bar. Two white-painted columns stood either side of the door. It wasn't unusual to see a row of scooters parked up alongside the pub up Mildmay Park.

Jack McVitie used to drink there 'til Reggie Kray hung his titfer up for him, permanently. The lads from Bethnal Green were regulars there and mods from across London came for the scene and to be seen. Those that were too young tried to. It wasn't easy to get in. You had to look sharp, the better dressed mods from across London, and Sean on the door kept out the riff-raff. Even if you got in, Jan the manager was not a woman to mess with and was quick to have people thrown out.

Ingrid was grooving to a sensational old sixties Joe Meek stomper: the Honeycombs' 'Have I the Right'. Still early doors and there was a group of girls, all dancing and all enjoying themselves. The punks had been doing the pogo, pose and robot for the last few years, dances that only barely gave any chance for sociability. The mods, though, loved to dance together. They celebrated their difference from the mundane. They enjoyed themselves, an eclectic mix of people, the array of music and moves as colourful as their Tootals and blazers.

Ingrid was half dancing with herself and half with a bright-eyed, young, mini-skirted mod girl called Marion. When one would do a new step or action, the other would watch from the side of their eye and then pick up on it 'til they were both moving in synchronicity. One would lean forward, the other back: keeping balance and harmony.

Dakin had other moves in mind. He'd been watching from the bar since Ingrid had entered the pub and taken to the dance floor. No sign of that lad Joe Bovver that was usually with her, an open goal?

He ordered a barley wine, for himself, and a Cinzano. Glasses in hand be moved onto the floor and nudged Ingrid on the elbow with his hand holding the drink he was offering.

'For you...' he indicated.

'What?' she queried with a puzzled look. The Little Roosters' 'I Need A Witness' had kicked in and was loud. Lovely, but loud.

Dakin gestured over to the bar, and taking the drink, she was hot, Ingrid followed him.

'I got you a drink,' he repeated.

'I've got it,' she responded. 'Thanks.' She thought him an oaf, but if Joe was cantankerous, it wouldn't hurt him to have a little competition. It'd either pull him closer or sort the situation out for good. She still hoped for the former, but she did need some fun in life.

He came on with the usual bunny. She nodded and laughed where she was expected to.

Thinking her a bit more mod than she actually was he'd asked her about bands, complimented her gear and barnet.

All a bit obvious for Ingrid, but she knew she looked the business. White jeans, powder-blue desert boots, and an open-collared Gabicci shirt striped in similar blues to her shoes. She'd had her hair done that day, and it still held its shape. Her fringe was long, and lined up just above the eyes, giving her an air of mystery, she thought. Heavy, black Dusty Springfield eyes added to the air, or maybe she'd been reading *Misty* comic too much. She'd dressed for dancing and being an east London girl, she never liked to look a two an' eight.

'You go to Alfredo's?' she was being asked.

She nodded. She did. It was a large caff on the Essex Road, the other end but not too far from the Mildmay. The café had been in the film

Quadrophenia that came out the previous year and since then mods ruled. Or at least the kids in their new-bought parkas plastered in sewn-on mod target patches thought they did. Alfredo's was one of London's better cafés and long been popular with the discerning cockney. It was getting difficult to get a decent egg and chips in there these days without some plum going on about the film.

'Wanna get something to eat there, with me?' Dakin was saying.

Why not? she thought. It was close, even better closed at this time of a Wednesday night so if she changed her mind she could just not turn up. Thinking she probably would show, it had the advantages of being public. She wasn't the sort to follow a bloke anywhere. The place had the advantage of not being too far from the manor, the food was good and she knew damn well that she'd get clocked there and word would get back to Joe.

He could either snap out of his moods or she'd do something about it. A sunny fried egg yolk is a beautiful thing but sooner or later the chip has to burst its pride.

CHAPTER 11

The cellar of the house Maria rented along with Susanne and Joanne was clean, but damp and decay were tangible in the air. The old houses around Brick Lane were dilapidated and without great demand, and, as a result, cheap. The windows had wooden shutters, to hide the rotten inside from the out, or the rotten outside from the in. The smell of fruit and veg from Spitalfields Market, just across Commercial Street, was rarely fresh and tramps had kept a smutty fire burning rubbish for years. Things hadn't changed much from the 1850s when Charles Manby Smith's *Curiosities of London Life* gave the opinion: 'Where the lark sung in the clouds, there is no ornithological utterance to be heard but that confounded chattering of impudent Cockney sparrows, which are invariably the first tenants to take possession of a London house, and are to its roof what, at a later period of its existence, the rats become to its cellars – a pest and a nuisance.'

The landlord was happy to rent to three good-looking girls. Despite all his weaselling no extras had come his way. None would.

A charcoal burner added a musk to the room, but the heavy smell of herbs was cloying rather than improving. The herbs had been gathered from Hackney Marshes and had brought the filthy, oily water of the River Lea with them. The odour they gave was noxious rather than nature. Maria had read the stories of Arthur Machen and paid special attention to the ones set in London. Machen had a feel for the creep of the city. His description of an old house in *Strange Occurrence in Clerkenwell* might have been for the very place she lived in, which was none too far from the same manor: 'the ancient clay, the dank reeking earth rising up again, and subduing all the work of men's hands after the conquest of many years.' She used incense particular to the work she was performing. Not only would it influence the spirit conjured but also it would encompass the room and magical tools. Maria breathed it in, making her one with the spirit and task. The density and fragrance was in affinity with, and attracted, the power she drew on and the result she willed to power.

The chalked circle on the floor within which Maria knelt didn't add any sense of life. Around its perimeter Hebrew words and arcane symbols were precisely drawn. At the four cardinal points things were placed. These were meant to draw in and channel what Maria was trying to achieve with this ritual. At the north: the skull and crossed leg bones of a dog. Maria was doing this to ensure the wolf curse passed from Joe to another. This circle was to focus and direct the spiritual energy and so it reflected the curse in its elements. A wolf skull would have been better but, in the London of 1980, these were not easy to obtain. To the east: a polished silver dish, representing the moon in all its might. This, though, was half covered with black velvet, to symbolise Joe being half-wolf, and only being himself when the moon was not full. The southern apex was a sprig of wolfsbane. The west: a fresh-killed jackdaw was laid, wings spread, prattle silenced, tongue agape as though a pathway to its soul.

Maria had snared this easily in the grounds of Hawksmoor's St Anne's Church in Limehouse. This spot where the rite had truly begun with her slashing the face of the wolf incarnate. The steeple of the church resembled the topmast of a ship, complete with crow's nest; it was built to be the first landmark sailors arriving in London would see. Sea captains would set their chronometers by its clock. The dead crow linked to that place, and being a crow, to the curse flying from one place to another.

Maria had her forehead pressed to the cold stone flags of the floor. Chanting 'Sator, Arepo, Tenet, Opera, Rotas', she lifted her shoulders and her head followed. She then parted her robe and laid the length of it around her. Some fine white chalk dusted the robe where it had brushed the floor.

Beneath it she was naked and freshly washed. A thin layer of oil gleamed on her skin. She reached into herself, down to the triangle at the centre of her being. Her fingers gently slipped into herself, and she began to work with finger and thumb on the nub of sensuality. Sensation began to wave through Maria's body, but rather than let it flood her mind, she kept her focus on the man and the wolf. The wolf is unrestrained lust and self-gratification; she could not allow herself that now. She needed to make use of the sexual tension as a tinder to the flame she would spark.

Sliding her hands up to her breasts, never losing contact with her smooth skin. She toyed with them, felt their give and take, luxuriating in their swing, heft and refusal to stay suppressed.

She was becoming all sensation, but kept the idea of the werewolf, and its transition, in her mind. Though she was taut with emotion, ready to burst with it, this was not for her own satisfaction, but to harness the energy of the rapture and release for her purpose.

Hands working faster and faster, her head rolled, hair loosening, breath rapid and short and not easy to catch. Beads of sweat ran between her breasts, they splattered from her oiled skin to the stone floor and stirred the dust of the chalked circle. Her fingers delved further and harder, she was frustrated that her knuckles limited how deep she could plumb. She rubbed faster, she wanted to give in to the pleasure, and was getting angry that the energy was focused on a man and not herself. How often had she had to end up finishing herself because men didn't know what they were doing, or weren't up to the task? Her dexterity was the opposite to their simplicity. She delved, caressed and cajoled. Her breath was coming shorter, her thighs danced and her back arched higher.

Once she had made her sacrifice of glory, her breath caught, a shudder ran through her spent body. She had built a cone of power. She could feel it throbbing around her, just as she could feel the echoing throb of muscle and passion within her. Before she could collapse into herself, she lifted the athame and pointed to the signs and sigils marked out within and around the circle. She directed the power: she had raised such, she now bid it to work.

This done, she let herself fall, exhausted, and drew deep breaths as the intensity left her and she took rest. She lay there some twenty minutes before the glow of her exertions expired and cold began to creep.

Stepping up, her feet padded across the stones. A different Maria Spiridonova left the cellar and made her way up to the warmth of her bedroom.

The electrickery of the light bulb coming on as Maria flicked the switch made for a completely different atmosphere. She divested herself of her robe and then opened the top drawer of a chest of drawers for clean underwear, always the top drawer for best. She took out a matching set of M&S powder-blue knickers and bra. These had a frill of lace to the hem. M&S: good quality, functional, rarely the potential for sauce but the meat and the gravy.

Taking a towel hanging from a hook on the back of the bedroom door she walked out to the hall and along to the bathroom. She put the plug firmly into the hole and then turned the hot tap briskly until it gushed. From the windowsill she took a jar of lavender-coloured bath salts and dashed some into the swirling waters. She then turned on the cold tap and leaned forward to mix the two.

Once clean, she took herself, wrapped in the towel, to her bedroom and started to dress in the underwear she'd left laid out on the bed. To brighten the mood still further, she hit play on a cassette recorder and reggae started playing. The cassette had been made for her by Ingrid and the choon was one of Joe's records: Earth & Stone's 'Why Girl', always the Joe Gibbs productions, that lad. She started to move in time to the regularity of the woodblock on the track. It was a 12-inch and she knew she could lose herself in it as she dressed.

There was some irony to the record she thought, a lovers' tune about loss. She'd be out to meet Joe and Mark soon, and with the ritual now complete everything was in place for Joe was close to seeing everything done.

She reached into her wardrobe for a mid-length royal-blue dress with a white Peter Pan collar but then thought 'pockets', pulled back and then went for a navy pair of ski-pants. Once in these she took a lemon twinset from a hanger. She wriggled into the short-sleeved jumper but then decided against the cardigan. She wouldn't need it. K Skips, the same yellow as the jumper, finished her. A quick check in the wardrobe mirror, keys and change in the tight hip pocket, and she was on her way.

It was a short walk to meet Joe and Mark at Dirty Dick's, past the rough trade brasses on Commercial Street and then along the side of Spitalfields Market down Brushfield Street. The pub was to the left then and opposite Liverpool Street station. Nathaniel Bentley, who'd opened the pub in 1761, was a real-life Miss Havisham. He'd been a dandy but the death of his fiancée on the eve of celebration of the wedding devastated him and he shut up the dining room of the house and became a miser, refusing to wash or clean. 'If I wash my hands today, they will be dirty again tomorrow', he was reputed to say. Much more punk than mod.

When she arrived Joe and Mark were sat in a dim corner. The pub still had a Dickensian dinginess to it. City boys were the main punters, drinking there before they got their trains back to Essex. One of the local bankers was already off his balance, he'd had a few and introduced himself: 'Hello. Doull. Julian Doull. Pint?' He was killing time 'til he had to get a train, but neither of the lads felt the need to be social. 'Whisky maybe?' he offered again.

Maria clocked all this as she slipped her way through the press at the bar. Joe had a boat as dour as Figgis in *Only When I Laugh*. Maria thought he needed cheering up so walked up to him and ran her finger below his nose saying, 'Guess who?' All it smelled of was bath salts, but Joe wasn't amused.

Mark stood to go and get the drinks in. He and Joe were nearly done with the one they'd been nursing but hadn't taken up the bloke on his drinks. Maria smiled coldly and Julian Doull made his way to the bar for another. Some people just don't know how to have a good time, he thought.

Mark was soon back. His new Bauhaus 'Dark Entries' t-shirt wasn't even remarked on. As soon as Maria had sat down Joe was pouring out that he'd heard about Ingrid eating in Alfredo's with Dakin.

'Did she arrive with him?' she asked.

Joe looked up from brimming pint and replied, 'I don't know?'

'You don't know,' Maria repeated slowly. 'Did she meet him there maybe?'

A shrug was the only response she got.

'Did they leave together? Alfredo's, so that was during the day, right?' she prodded.

'Yeah, yeah,' Joe nodded. 'Just the caff. But I ain't best pleased.'

'This is good,' Maria said, prodding him in the shoulder with her same finger. 'This is what you need.'

Joe looked dejected.

'Nothing's happened,' reassured Maria as Mark returned with two of the three drinks. 'That girl's well into you. If that tosser Dakin is on her case, then all wolfery is gonna bite him. He just needs to take it.

'Don't,' prod, 'go,' prod, 'soft,' prod, 'now.'

Maria took a sip of her snowball. 'It's the Rejects in a couple of weeks, innit?'

Joe and Mark both nodded.

'He'll be there, you can bet that,' she continued. She was excitedly dancing about in her chair and rubbing her hands. 'We'll all be there: you, Ingrid, me, him. Oh, everything is coming together.'

CHAPTER 12

Everyone was meeting at the top of Stamford Hill, at the crossroads with Clapton Common to one side and Amhurst Park to the other. They were going into Camden Town, always lively of a Saturday. They'd all get the 253 bus that traversed the broad main roads, past Finsbury Park, then Holloway Prison, 'til it got to Camden Town. Joe was still after 'Fally Ranking', the Greensleeves 12 that was killing in dances. Camden was good for records, not especially reggae but Rock On might have a copy. Ingrid and her mate Joyce were both after clothes, punk and mod styles were plentiful on the market stalls there. Compendium Books was also gonna get a visit. Joe loved reading and this particular bookshop had books you'd not find anywhere else in London. The people who ran the shop were kosher, they'd frequently give a young chelloveck a good steer.

Ingrid liked a book, too. Like Joe she knew that nothing terrifies the upper classes as much as a knowledgeable oik. She didn't buy too many, Joe always had heaps of them piled up beside his bed.

The red Routemaster bus was rickety, but

reliable. They crammed in, two to a seat, at the back of the bus. It being shabbes there weren't too many other people boarding. The top deck smelled of stale cigarette smoke. Joe wasn't a smoker. It often annoyed him he'd wear decent gear out and it'd come back pen and inking. There was a lad near the front of the bus eating a Cornish pasty. It must have been red-hot because he was doing so slowly, and the smell of the pastry, meat and carrots mingled with that of the tobacco.

Joe sat back and could feel the brush of the fabric on the seat; municipal fabric, standard and hard-wearing on the buses and tubes, though often with worn patches from the hundreds of arses that sat on it daily. Joe was wearing jungle greens, army surplus trousers with a fresher green than the usual drab olive that had a couple of nice details: buttoned belt loops and a generous back pocket. There was also an oversized flapped pocket between the hip and knee on the left. The Army & Navy Stores in Forest Gate did a brisk trade in them to builders, punks, and skinheads. The trendier army surplus shop did good business with 'em, too, at Laurence Corner, just down the Hampstead Road towards Euston.

Joe's were hemmed to the sixth eye of eight-hole cherry reds. Ingrid's mate Nina had a new sewing machine and had started a little business making pinafore dresses and the like for the mod girls on the manor from patterns her mum had left over from the sixties. Turning up trousers was easy for her.

Most of the journey was taken up with talk of the Cockney Rejects gig the following weekend. Everyone wanted to go, and it looked to be an exciting one. Eventually the bus rattled to a halt at the right stop and Joe, Ingrid, Joyce, Porky and Mark thundered down the curve of the stairs and out onto the street. They dodged the traffic over the busy Camden Road and ran the short distance to the Rock On record shop which nestled close to Camden Town tube. Next door to that was Holt's shoe shop. Joe nudged Ingrid's elbow and gave his head a nod indicating that he was going in there.

Holt's had a fine array of Loakes brogues and loafers, the squarer, less elaborate (and better) Frank Wright loafers, and especially Dr Martens. Since he was a saucepan, Joe had been getting his shoes from Blackman's on Brick Lane. While at Holt's you could walk in and get the style you wanted in the size you wanted, Blackman's worked on a 'what we've got, we've got' basis. You might not get what you went in there for, but you'd get a decent pair of shoes and at a good price.

For today Joe was just after a pair of yellow bootlaces. They weren't much of themselves but it's the small details that make style. The yellow stood out against the cherry red of a shined pair and brought up the yellow stitching holding the sole to the body of the boot. They tended to pick up the polish from when you antiqued your boots, so Joe went through quite a few pairs of laces to keep himself looking sharp.

These in pocket, they all crammed into the shoebox crush of Rock On. The small record shop was packed full of soul, R&B, punk and reggae records and all the ingredients thereof. Porky had his Levi jacket unbuttoned to display his Madness t-shirt. He was, as always, after badges. His pocket flaps were always a shmeer of 2 Tone, punk, RAR, reggae, the buttons of a non-stop mental jukebox. He rushed straight to the counter and was looking at those pinned behind hoping there was something new. While Joyce and Mark were poring over the cover of the new Cabaret Voltaire album, Joe was flipping through a rack of reggae 12s. There were a few Greensleeves records there, Ingrid could see from their distinctive 'carnival of reggae' sleeves, complete with skinheads, but she could also tell by the strop Joe was getting on that 'Fally Ranking' wasn't one of 'em.

'You got "Fally Ranking" in?' Joe shouted over to the counter.

'Nah, son. That's selling fast. We'll have more in the week.'

Definitely annoyed now, Joe walked out of the shop and waited while Joyce paid for the Cabs album. He was facing the Mother Red Cap pub opposite. The pub was built over the home of a witch, Mother Damnable. Witches, curses, portents seemed to hem Joe in every way.

Once everyone was out on the street they turned to the right and followed through the tube station and along to Camden Market.

'I'm gonna be looking at clothes, you go look at books. I'll see you at the Dublin Castle and we can all have a beer,' Ingrid suggested to Joe.

He nodded and continued through the madding crowd along to Compendium, sat just before the Regent's Canal bridge.

Just past the jumble of stalls Joe glanced into the window of the Bucks Head pub. Dakin was sat having a beer. Both were surprised to see the other and Dakin immediately put finger and thumb together and gesticulated: 'wanker'. Joe wasn't fazed, blew a kiss and continued on.

He thought Dakin might follow him out for a dig but knew the one thing that repulsed prats was books and kept on keeping on.

Compendium was jam-packed with books. The street window had an array of interesting, and unusual, titles and then the three walls around were piled high with titles you'd have trouble finding anywhere else in London.

True enough, there was a long-standing occult bookshop by the British Museum that Joe had gone to after talking to Mark and Maria, but the proprietor dyed his hair raven, and Joe thought if he did that, the magic he was punting must be pony.

Joe usually bought zines and history books in the shop. It amused, and delighted, the staff he picked up a mix of high- and low-brow. There's something of the well-dressed skinhead in that.

He often chatted with Liz Young, an erudite and engaging punk who worked there. She'd steered him onto some useful books on anarchism during the Russian revolution, as well as some decent zines. She'd been the Clash's Mick Jones' girlfriend and had a similar taste in music.

Ray Gange has a toilet moment with her in the film *Rude Boy* that was in the cinemas earlier that year. 'Don't call me love, I don't believe in it,' Ray tells her. She doesn't and ditches him first chance she gets.

Liz and Joe had some lively conversation and, after he'd perused the shelves, she recommended a box set of the Robert Graves Claudius books that the shop had in. Both *I, Claudius* and *Claudius the God* in a sturdy box with a mosaic picture on the front that Penguin had put out for the compelling BBC series a couple of years ago. Joe had enjoyed that, John Hurt as Caligula had been especially funny, and chilling. With that, and Liz's nod, he handed over the required. He also rolled a copy of *Jamming* in his pocket. There were interviews in the zine with the Selecter and The Jam, both bands with something to say.

With the ring of the till in his ears he set off the way he'd come to meet the others at the Dublin Castle, up on Parkway. Slightly off the market but a favourite for people who liked music.

As he'd worried, Dakin was now outside the Bucks Head. From a few yards away they locked eyes as Joe walked steadily forward.

'What's with the kiss? You some sort of ir–' Dakin spat but was halted abruptly as Joe slammed the spine of the box set of books into the bridge of Dakin's nose.

The cartilage gave way and shut Dakin up mid-word as pain starred through him and his eyes welled. Remembering an apt John Hurt line from *I, Clavdivs*, where Caligula has just killed his wife and blamed his best friend for it, Joe chuckled, 'Aren't people *awful*?' and kept right on walking.

Dakin was left on the street, people making their way round him, as the pain intensified and focused, his nose spotting like an old dripper. Five splashes of blood fell to the floor. Five points of the pentagram.

CHAPTER 13

The next night was a full moon, and the proximity was making Joe anxious. The silver pentagram itched against his chest. He was walking towards the bus stop, Blakeys on his shoes announcing him with a stern clack, sounding to Joe like the dread ticking of a clock.

Ahead of him, just by the flats with the ubiquitous 'No Ball Games' signs, a half-dozen kids were creeping with exaggerated caution up to a woman pushing a sturdy pram who pretended not to notice them. Once they were close, they'd yell, 'What's the time, Mister Wolf?'

The mum would reply, 'Ten o'clock.' 'Eleven o'clock', until the moment she yelled, 'Dinner time!' and the kids ran delightedly screaming past Joe and the mum grimaced and held up her hands, fingers bent as claws.

She smiled as she saw Joe, he smiled back but the moment gave him some unease. He sat wondering on the bus if this was a portent, and of all that Maria had said about the time for Mr Wolf being over.

The gig was already filling. Lads were trying to look tough, girls alluring. All their boat races as described by occultist Dion Fortune in *The Return of the Ritual*: 'irregular Cockney features.' The punks had spiked their hair, skinheads freshly cropped their barnets. T-shirts had been carefully chosen to make statements and pledge the right allegiance. Dr Marten had faithful followers. The Glory Boys, hard East End mod faces who used to follow Secret Affair but were now to be seen at Cockney Rejects gigs, had a corner of the bar to themselves. The space came from a well-earned reputation. They were better turned out than most, not sporting any of the potato-print tat for sale at the Last Resort down Petticoat Lane. Their mod look edged to suedehead, away from the scruff of punk that many of the boots and braces skins maintained.

The atmosphere was already alive with expectation. The Rejects were a Bash Street Kids ruckus of a band who played raucous punk; yobs like us centre stage, always a chance of aggro. The gigs like the football, like the pubs, like the streets.

Tight gangs of young skinheads prowled, chests puffed out. Disparate mobs eyed one another, different manor, football team, plain antagonism all added edge to the taut atmosphere.

Joe was in a tasty large-check red gingham button-down, tonik trousers, red socks and oxblood Loakes brogues. Trousers rarely lasted longer than a jacket, some people bought two pairs for a whistle. Many a skinhead got the most from a whistle by wearing a decent tonik jacket; ticket pockets, pocket square, pocket stud, with a pair of pressed, turned-up 501s and antiqued daisies once the kaffies had gone for a Burton.

He'd eschewed wearing a t-shirt, the skinhead 'look' was getting obvious as it was veering to a high-street fashion. Why be exactly as people thought you were when you can be something more, was Joe's opinion.

Dakin was a case in point, leaning on the bar on the opposite side, and the opposite of style in predictable boots, braces and 'Out of Control' t-shirt. He was giving Joe ice picks but staying put, Joe was chatting to a couple of Glory Boys. He knew 'em as the mod zine *Maximum Speed* from '79 had a Stamford Hill address and he'd bought copies at gigs and football. Dakin knew not to trouble trouble and, for now, was content to give it the big 'un rather than deliver. He was also wondering if Joe was with these lads, where was Ingrid? Was she on her Jack?

Ingrid was on the left of the crowd packed in to see Canning Town's finest. Maria, Porky, Mark and her were a tight redcoat square. She was still miffed at Joe, he'd been an arse recently, but at least he'd brought her out to the gig that everyone wanted to be at.

Mark had been hanging out with Ingrid a lot over the last few weeks. They were mates, but he was also acting as a buffer between her and Joe telling her everything. Mark and Maria knew how much they meant to each other, if she knew what Joe was going through, she'd want to help and sympathise. With her cleaving to Joe the curse would never be taken. Joe had to love her enough to be prepared to let her go, otherwise the wolf would end up slashing through everything in his life, her included.

The lights dimmed and then burst as the Cockney Rejects' teenage singer bounded onto stage, grabbed the mic and yelled, 'All right, John!' The band pounded into the introduction of their song 'East End', both celebration and two-fingered defiance, the crowd immediately joined in with terrace-style handclaps, bouncing and singing along.

From that moment the front of the crowd was mayhem. The bodies of excited yoofs pressed together against the front of the stage. The kids were leaping, pushing each other and shouting along to the songs. The nebulousness of the energy being released delighted Maria, all the more that there was so much tanked-up teenage testosterone with thumbs behind its braces.

Dakin barged his way through the outer edges towards Ingrid and her mates. He was all elbows and continued 'til he inserted himself between Ingrid and Mark. Cupping his hand, the interloper yelled, 'Good, innit?' into her ear. She gave a puzzled look as if she couldn't hear a thing over the band and the ebullient crowd. Dakin was getting intrusively into her space, so she leaned back.

Joe clocked this from the bar at the back of the hall. He'd had enough of Dakin giving it the big 'un, especially where Ingrid was concerned. Weaving his way through knots of kids jumping up and down to the band, he made his way over.

He grabbed Dakin's shoulder and pulled him back. Dakin swung quickly round to see who was giving him ag'. Seeing it was Joe, seeing he was on his own, and wanting to look hard in front of Ingrid, he gave Joe a shove in the chest that knocked him a few steps back. The smooth soles of Joe's brogues weren't helping but just as they were finding traction he slid through a pool of beer slopped from some eager punk's pint. He wheeled comically trying to find footing, like a moment from *Scooby-Doo*.

Dakin pointed and laughed, Ingrid looked away, Joe fumed.

'You're nish, a bleedin' doughnut 'ole,' Dakin mocked. Joe could barely hear what was being said, the band were in full sway, but he knew it couldn't be anything complimentary.

Still off-kilter he moved to Dakin, thinking to plant a hook on Dakin's jaw but the uneven footing and his arm swinging out unbalanced him more. The move had been telegraphed and Dakin saw it coming a mile off, side-stepped and gave Joe a slap to the cheek.

The slap was more demeaning than a punch, meant to publicly belittle, and the slight force of it sent him down to the floor in a jumble of arms and legs. He lifted himself onto one knee in order to stand up again. As he did so Dakin leaned over him and bowed, regally.

Joe was burning with rage now, fire sparked in his eyes, he was aching to plant his fists.

The band were on their third song, the suppressed chords of the guitar building the tension.

Over Dakin's shoulder Maria and Mark were staring intently at Joe. Maria was moving her hands in a 'stay down' gesture. She realised that this could be the moment they'd been working towards. All Dakin had to do now was to take from Joe.

Joe rose slowly, the slops from the floor messing the knees of his trousers. The slap had left a vivid red handprint on his cheek.

Dakin leaned in closely and laughed ostentatiously in his face.

Maria was now waving her hands back and forth. 'Do nothing,' she was mouthing to Joe, 'DO NOTHING.'

The guitar, bass and drums were building up.

'You ain't nuffink,' Dakin said again.

'I'm gonna have a pop, I'm going to have your bird, and...' Dakin stretched out his arm and quickly snatched the hanging silver amulet that had tumbled out of Joe's shirt when he'd fallen, '... I'm gonna have this.'

Dakin tugged and the chain holding the pentagram around Joe's neck snapped. The five-pointed star was firm in Dakin's grasp as he pulled his arm back.

Joe could see why Maria and Mark had been telling him to do nothing now. Hope started to run through him. Would all that Maria had said follow?

The band reached the chorus and the guitars swept into a release. The crowd, previously a suspicious mix of football firms and manors, now joined as one voice to chant communally along.

Dakin saw Joe smile and was puzzled. He shouldn't be doing that.

A surge of power shocked from the silver clutched in his hand. It raced through Dakin, all the trains from the bottle at the heart of the tube map rushing to the outreaches. He reeled back, confused. Just when he'd made Joe look a loser, why was the fucker grinning so? Why was he feeling knocked sideways? He hadn't had a single punch land on him, and he'd only had a couple of pints. What... the... hell?

CHAPTER 14

A weal the shape of a pentagram rapidly rose on Dakin's palm. He started to reel and staggered into the manic mob focused on the Rejects. His eyes burned yellow, every hair on his body stood erect. He felt like he wanted to come, shit and puke all at the same time. There's probably some German porno that shows just that.

His muscles rippled and he lost sway over his arms and legs as a fresh potency poured through them. It felt like a rush of speed, but Dakin didn't remember taking any. The come-down was quicker, too, the come-down was coming now.

His arms thrashed, he was bent double, legs tottering. He blundered into the throng of kids pressing up to the stage as the Rejects powered on. A fist he had no control over smashed into the cheek of a young skinhead. Then the other punched into the stomach of another as his arms writhed and he edged slowly forward, crouching, further and further.

This was not a gig to start in, everyone here was ready to ruck. The skinhead who'd caught the first punch turned and kicked. The kick landed, but

Dakin felt nothing. Him not registering just caused the skinhead to kick him again all the harder.

He was not transforming to the wolf, not yet, but the curse was coursing. The beast was settling into the marrow of his bones, the fibres of his being. Initially he was impervious to the blows landing from the outraged skinheads around him. Kicks, then punches. As a werewolf he'd be stronger, quicker and more vicious than anyone. But he was not one to one; he was in the midst of a pack.

The first skinhead was still kicking, then the second he'd lashed out at was on him with a flurry of blows. These landed unfelt but more thugs joined, throwing wild punches, their boots landing into the mass of writhing youth, faces contorted with random hate. Some managed to kick Dakin, some boots landed on others, no one was that concerned. Music and dancing are fun, but this was the release they craved.

Kids nearby darted out of the way of the developing ruck, some were eager to join in. Dakin started to wither under the weight of battering. His ribs and face had taken a pummelling; blood began to seep from his bruised face. He tried to crawl forward, stand upright, fight back, but the skinhead moonstomp was too much. Again and again the boots stamped down. He collapsed, unable to take any more but the boots were relentless.

Soles of the oil-, fat-, acid-, petrol-, alkali-resistant boots landed on the hand clutching the spent amulet.

The hand opened as bones cracked and the pentagram was sent skittering into the crowd. A teenage girl with black spiky hair, too much dark make-up and a 'Bela Lugosi's Dead' t-shirt cinched with a studded leather belt saw the silver sparkling, reached down and picked it up. She briefly looked at it and slipped it in her pocket. It looked suitably spooky for her aesthetic.

Bouncers came rushing through the crowd. Burly blokes who pushed the kicking knot of kids aside. They grabbed the dazed Dakin by his collar and dragged him to the back of the hall. A smear of blood marked his course.

Excitement over and not wanting to be slung out, the skinheads scattered into the crowd and went back to losing themselves to the band.

Maria was at Joe's side watching it all unfold. 'See... I told you!'

Joe already felt so much better, both in himself and at Dakin's demise. There was a gleam back in his eye. Maria and Mark had offered some hope, but that was always outweighed by doubt. Here, though, at last, he was free of the curse, free to be who he really was, free to be with the girl he loved.

*

This Saturday, being a full moon, Joe did not have to journey out to the sticks. He's invited Ingrid round to his. He'd even tidied up. A bit.

He'd picked up the dirty plates left by the side of his bed and washed them. The little mophead on a stick did more work in half an hour than it had in the last month. He'd also taken the books scattered there and shelved them. He made sure that Colin MacInnes was prominent. He'd not read all of the London trilogy but so far was loving what he had. There was just *Mr Love and Justice* to go.

Joe's shirts were always hung neatly in his wardrobe, no wire hangers. The one he'd wear out of a particular evening on a wooden hanger hung from the front of wardrobe to one side of the long central mirror. The rest of his gear was left to suffer. The clothes, pants and socks mostly, were picked up from the floor and put in the laundry hamper. He made sure his best pair of pants sat at the top of the pile in his underwear drawer. What's good ain't called top drawer for nothing and he couldn't be sure that Ingrid wouldn't look in there for some reason.

As he was lifting a pair of Sta-Prest he remembered an odd bit in the *Satyricon*; during Trimalchio's dinner a tale is told whereby someone sheds their clothes in a graveyard, pisses a ring around them and turns into a wolf. Joe put the thought from mind, and the trousers in to be laundered.

He turned his TV on to keep him company 'til Ingrid arrived. A film double bill was just starting, Lon Chaney's *The Wolf Man*. Joe's heart sank. This was really not what he needed. To make it even worse the following one was *Werewolf of London*. The old black-and-white Universal horrors are great but these two in particular were really not what he needed.

To brighten his mood, he grabbed the first record from the stack against his bookcase and slapped it on the deck, the needle found the groove to Barrington Levy's 'Quick Divorce'. He'd invited Ingrid round to ensure there'd be no such break-up. Could have chosen better, he thought.

The door bell suddenly rang insistently and he started. It wasn't unexpected but it burst into his train of thought. He gave the room a quick scan, nothing amiss, and then went down the short flight of stairs to the ground floor to let Ingrid in. He smiled, planted a big kiss on her, and told her she looked nice, and she did.

'Aren't you the Edward Fox,' she stated.

He more than owed her some niceness, he well knew.

They trotted upstairs and Ingrid caught the end of Lui Lepke's DJing on the choon. 'Saying something?' she enquired pointedly of Joe.

'No... no,' he stuttered. 'Look, I know I've been a bit of a dick for a while. I won't be again. Well... as much.'

'What was up? It had better be about you and not me,' Ingrid made clear.

'Call it my time of the month,' Joe proffered.

'Well, it had better be over,' she responded.

'I promise.' Joe moved to her and put his arms around her, hugging her close. He kissed the top of her head. 'I promise.'

'Well, I've got you something if that's the case,' Ingrid said. She'd brought a brown Adidas holdall with her, and this was at her feet. She reached in and pulled out a brown paper bag with a couple of records inside. 'I got these today,' she told Joe. 'There's a couple for me and one for you.'

She pulled the Greensleeves 12 of 'Fally Ranking' out of the bag and gave it to Joe with a smile. His face lit up. Things with her were getting sorted and the record he'd been after for weeks. Joy. After weeks of hiding his feelings, it felt so good to be able to let them out into the daylight. Ingrid warmed to his beaming face. She could see it was genuine happiness and that was something she wanted them both to share.

'Barrington has said all he's gonna say,' Ingrid affirmed. 'Put that on and dance with me. Then you can fix me a coffee.'

They held each other close, physically and emotionally. The dance was the moment, the steps were the future.

Once the record had played out Ingrid flopped down on the bed. Joe made eyes, but she firmly said, 'Coffee.'

'I dreamed about you last night,' Joe whispered.

'Did you...'

'No, you wouldn't let me.'

Ingrid chuckled. She was glad to see his sulkiness was over, and happy to feel wanted again. She'd had her doubts over the past few weeks.

He unscrewed the pot, poured water into the base, tapped the ground coffee into the funnel, put it all together and onto the stove. As he was caught in the ritual of it, Ingrid put one of her records on: gentle, plaintive, but ultimately brutal: the Young Marble Giants' 'Final Day'. Joe was caught by minimal music and the clean, beautiful voice. There was an end to things, but this was a beginning just as much. The moon was not liming yet, but when it did it would shine though Joe's window onto his bed. The couple might stay in for the night, they might go out, come back then wake together, at last there was a choice; for them both.

It was gorgeous and delicious. Ingrid dropped the song again, Joe looked over to her as she took the couple of steps from the record player to his bed. He could picture himself there, next to Ingrid, arms around her. He could give the moon. The record played short, but not racing. The singing was lovely and so was what they would soon do together. The climax was still to come. He was cured all right.

ACKNOWLEDGEMENTS

Thanks to: Misty, Phill Jupitus, Peyvand Sadeghian, Rhoda Dakar, Paul Putner, Guen Murroni, The Betsey Trotwood, Cathi Unsworth, The Ruts, Clare Pollard, John Mitchinson, Angela Mao, Tighten Up Crew, Delinquent Girl Boss, Joel Loya, Dublin's finest, Hard As Nails, Richard Boon, Werewolf Beer, The Dangerfields, Mrs Elswood, Hammer House of Horror, Stewart Lee, Boots-N-Booze, friends and family, Johnny Alucard, New English Library, and all of the *Pan Book of Horror Stories*.

Unbound is the world's first crowdfunding publisher, established in 2011.

We believe that wonderful things can happen when you clear a path for people who share a passion. That's why we've built a platform that brings together readers and authors to crowdfund books they believe in – and give fresh ideas that don't fit the traditional mould the chance they deserve.

This book is in your hands because readers made it possible. Everyone who pledged their support is listed below. Join them by visiting unbound.com and supporting a book today.

Jabari Adisa
Glenn Airey
Mick Albers
Johnny Alucard
John Baine
Jason Ballinger
Eric Barnes
Graham Barnfield
Paul Barrett
Michael Baxter

Russ Bestley
Wendy May Billingsley
Alister Black
Sophia Blackwell
Michael Bolger
Ed Bonilla
Richard Boon
Stuart Borthwick
Danny Bowyer
Richard Brass

Nick Bray
Annie Brechin
Timothy Brown
Crystal Brownfield
Gary Budden
Garry Bushell
Chris Butler
Paul Carlyle
Paul Case
Liam Casey
Rebecca Charlton
Andy Ching
Vera Chok
Sadeka Choudhuri
Juan Christian
James Clark
Tom Claydon
Mathew Clayton
Emma Cole
Mark Coverdale
Stella Coyle
Peter Coyte
Sean Cregan
Ian Crisp
Tom Cullen
Rich Davenport
Katy Derbyshire
Jamie Dobson
Ryan Down

Tony Drayton
Stef Duke
Donal Dunne
Bobby Durnan –
    forever loved R.I.P. ♥
John Eden
Travis Elborough
Roxanne Escobales
Christian Evans
Jonathan Eyre
Pete Fender
Jessica Fenn
Julian Fenton
Clare Ferguson-Walker
Ged Forrest
Martin Fransén
Steven Friel
Roual Galloway
Ray Gange
Katja Gaude
Salena Godden
Michael Goodwin
Don Gosh
Ian Greensmith
Michael Haber
Amy Hall
Paul Hallam
Chip Hamer
Davinia Hamilton

Glyn Harries
Mark Harris
Ella Harrison
Martin Harrison
Neil Harrison
Simon Haynes
Merrill Heatley
Kenneth Hellman
Lisa Henderson
Keiron Higgins
Bob Hill
Brendan 'Cod Eyes'
    Hodges
Gary Horsman
Colin Hoskin
Geraint Hughes
Mark Hynds
Cian Hynes
Andy Jackson
Walt Jensen
Richard Jones
Phill Jupitus
Natalie Katsou
Pete Keeley
Christopher Kellogg
Janet Kelly
Dan Kieran
Julian King
Sarah Kobrinsky

Allan Lauder
Stewart Lee
Alain Letarte
Simon Lidgate
Ital Lion
Charlie Longman
Polly Love
Joel Loya
Bernard Mahon
Gita Malhotra
Joe Manning
Angela Mao
Soozin Marshall
Martin Mathers
Yvonne Carol McCombie
Kate McCrimmon
Liam McGurk
Michael McLaughlin
John Mitchinson
Suzanne Moore
Gavin Moorhead
Katrina Moseley
Taff Mowatt
Gordon Munro
Luke J Murray
Guen Murroni
Carlo Navato
Andrew Neilson
Lee Nelson

Karen Nixon

Jan Noble

Sean O'Brien

Caoimhe O'Gorman

Niall O'Sullivan

Gema Oliver

John Osborne

Tim Paine

Daniel Paris-Clavel

Gary Patterson

Scottish Paul

Peter Phipps

Marco Pirroni

Ingrid Pitt

Phil Platt

Clare Pollard

Justin Pollard

Gareth Postans

Richard Prangle

Suzy Prince

Paul Putner

Nick Pyne

Cina Qedesh

Sam Quill

Zoran Radicheski

Pete Raynard

Marc Read

Gary Riley

Dale 'ROBBO' Robertson

Micheal Roche

Nick Rothstein

Mark Rourke

Liberty Rowley

David Rumsey

Deborah Scordo Mackie

Mark Scott

Jon Seagrave

Scott Seath

Heidi Seppälä

Jaimie Shorten

Henrik Sjögren

Joe Skade

Craig Skinner

Angela Smith

Martin Smyth

Mazzy Snape

Mike Spex

Ross Sutherland

Claire Tarbox

Carl Taylor

The Betsey Trotwood

The Squire

Frank Theis

Guy Thompson

Tonic Sta Press

Tim Turnbull

Colin Udall

John Vaccaro

Becky Varley-Winter
Liz Vater
Julie Vee
Vout-O-Reenees
Becky Walker
Melissa Walker
Julie Warren
Veronica Warry
Sarah Wells
Kim West

Rich White
Steve White
Tony White
Jacob Wilson
Lucy Wood
Darryl Woollaston
Matthew Worley
Maor Yavetz
Susie Yavetz

Bestsellers in this Library

Scares and Slippers – Tim Wells
Little Witch – Victoria Park
12HexU – Cathi Punsworth
Love In Pain – Barry Gudden
Hairy Manners – JK Appalling
There There My Fear – James Bell
Beast Friend – Honour Chen-Williams
Terror in the Bathroom – Herbert James
Stalking Down the Kings Road – Gill Brundy
Another Ghoul Another Planet – Herrill Meatley